DARK ENEMY CAPTIVE

THE CHILDREN OF THE GODS BOOK 5

I. T. LUCAS

FOLLOW I. T. LUCAS ON AMAZON

THE CHILDREN OF THE GODS

THE CHILDREN OF THE GODS ORIGINS

1: GODDESS'S CHOICE

2: GODDESS'S HOPE

THE CHILDREN OF THE GODS

DARK STRANGER

1: DARK STRANGER THE DREAM

2: DARK STRANGER REVEALED

3: DARK STRANGER IMMORTAL

DARK ENEMY

4: DARK ENEMY TAKEN

5: DARK ENEMY CAPTIVE

6: DARK ENEMY REDEEMED

KRI & MICHAEL'S STORY

6.5: MY DARK AMAZON

DARK WARRIOR

7: DARK WARRIOR MINE

8: DARK WARRIOR'S PROMISE

9: DARK WARRIOR'S DESTINY

10: DARK WARRIOR'S LEGACY

Dark Guardian

11: Dark Guardian Found

12: Dark Guardian Craved

13: Dark Guardian's Mate

Dark Angel

14: Dark Angel's Obsession

15: Dark Angel's Seduction

16: Dark Angel's Surrender

Dark Operative

17: Dark Operative: A Shadow of Death

18: Dark Operative: A Glimmer of Hope

19: Dark Operative: The Dawn of Love

Dark Survivor

20: Dark Survivor Awakened

21: Dark Survivor Echoes of Love

22: Dark Survivor Reunited

Dark Widow

23: Dark Widow's Secret

24: Dark Widow's Curse

25: Dark Widow's Blessing

TRY THE SERIES ON

AUDIBLE

2 FREE audiobooks with your new Audible subscription!

NOTE FROM THE AUTHOR:
This is a work of fiction!

Names, characters, places and incidents are products of the
author's imagination or are used fictitiously and are not to be
construed as real. Any similarity to actual persons, organizations
and/or events is purely coincidental.

CONTENTS

CHAPTER 1: ANDREW

*A*s the chopper began to descend, Andrew turned to the window and watched the bright helipad square on Kian's rooftop grow closer. There was a big letter A in its center that he hadn't noticed upon takeoff, and Andrew wondered what it stood for.

An A for Amanda? An A for awesome immortals?
Should be an F for fucking unbelievable...

The moment the craft touched down, Syssi rushed out from the cover of the vestibule onto the open rooftop—a gust of wind catching her long hair and blowing it around her head in a mad swirl. It looked like she was cold—the poor girl huddled inside her light jacket, tucking her chin and holding the collar against her cheeks.

That got her boyfriend moving fast.

With a muted curse, Kian threw the passenger's door open and jumped down. Ducking under the chopper's slowing blades, he ran out and wrapped his arms around Syssi.

It was good that the guy's wide back obscured what must've been a passionate kiss. As much as Andrew approved of Syssi's boyfriend, it didn't mean that he was okay with seeing his kid sister engaged in anything even remotely sexual.

It must have been pure hell for Kian to find Amanda as he had—spread out naked in postorgasmic bliss. Lucky for Andrew, he'd gotten on the scene a couple of minutes later, missing the main act of her and the Doomer getting it on.

It seemed to be his thing lately. He'd also been spared Syssi's almost fatal transition, learning about it only after the fact.

Thank God, she'd pulled through.

It was better that he hadn't been there. He would've gone crazy from worry and would've attacked Kian—consequences be damned. Someone must be watching over him, shielding him from stuff he couldn't stomach.

Though before shit had gone down at the cabin, Andrew had seen enough through the Xaver imaging equipment. He'd gotten more than an eyeful while scanning the cabin's interior. Thank God for the electromagnetic radar's crappy, pixelated display.

Unfortunately, the picture hadn't been hazy enough...

Fuck, he'd better not go there if he wanted to keep his shit together.

Besides, it was none of his business. Amanda was a big girl and could do whatever she pleased with whomever she chose—even if it was a scumbag Doomer who didn't deserve to lick the crap off the bottom of her shoes.

Andrew had no claim on her—of any kind.

Not yet.

God, seeing her naked had been like an electric shock. It had scrambled his brain and had refocused it into a singular objective—making this spectacular woman his. But he would've preferred not to have shared the experience with a bunch of other guys. Thank you very much.

The immortals he could've tolerated. After all, Kian was her brother and his bodyguards were her cousins. But not Rodney and Jake, Andrew's own buddies. After the many years they had served together, the two were like brothers to him, but that didn't mean he'd been okay with them drooling over Amanda.

His only consolation was that they would remember nothing of tonight. Including Amanda's perfect, nude body. Before heading out, they had agreed to let Kian erase the whole rescue mission from their memories upon their return.

Andrew sneaked a glance at Syssi and Kian, hoping they were done with the kissing. Damn. Not only were their mouths still fused together in a heated smooch, but Kian had lifted Syssi and was trying to carry her inside.

An argument ensued, and she pushed at his chest in a futile attempt to make him put her down. After some more back and forth, it seemed a compromise had been reached. Syssi stayed outside, and Kian wrapped himself around her like a human coat. Well, not really human, close enough though.

Even when idling, the helicopter's engine was too loud to hear the particulars of their argument, but it had been easy to get the gist of it just by observing their body language. And it was obvious that Syssi had the big guy wrapped around her little finger.

Good, so Andrew wasn't the only one who was putty in her hands.

He'd learned a long time ago that his sweet kid sister's shy and demure demeanor was misleading. Syssi never backed down from what was important to her and somehow managed to bend even the toughest and the meanest to her will.

How did the saying go? The bigger they were, the harder they fell?

True, that.

Andrew smiled, glad that the lovebirds were getting along so well.

Kian was a wise man if he'd already discovered the magic of the two most important words in a guy's vocabulary—*yes, dear.*

As soon as Amanda stepped down and took a few steps away from the helicopter, Syssi discarded the sheltering arms of her boyfriend and ran to hug her friend.

Evidently, that hug was exactly what Amanda needed, and long moments passed as the women stood in each other's arms.

It pained Andrew to see Amanda's shoulders heave as she cried in Syssi's embrace. The woman had abandoned her tough act at the first sign of loving compassion.

Kian was such a self-absorbed colossal jerk. Would it have killed him to give Amanda a hug?

When the heaving finally stopped, Amanda let go and swept a finger under her teary eyes. Casting a baleful glance at Kian, Syssi wrapped her arm around Amanda's waist and together they walked inside.

Andrew had a feeling the big guy was going to sleep in the proverbial doghouse tonight. Not that he didn't deserve it for treating Amanda like shit— regardless of the extenuating circumstances.

Judging by the murderous expression on Kian's

face, he was well aware of his unfavored status, and Andrew was not going to let him mess with Rodney and Jake's memories until he had a chance to calm down.

The plan was to leave them with a memory of going on an unspecified, top-secret mission they'd agreed to be hypnotized to forget. It wasn't perfect, but the guys had to have a rational explanation, or they'd think they were losing their freaking minds. As it was, it would have been hard enough to explain the missing day. Explaining the large sum of money magically showing up in their bank accounts would have been even more difficult.

But until he made sure Kian was up to the task, Andrew's buddies would keep Brundar and Anandur company and wait in the chopper for the gurney to transport the prisoner to the dungeon.

How cool was it that they had a fucking dungeon down in their basement? Just to get a gander at that, he would've volunteered to escort the prisoner himself.

But he had to keep an eye on Kian while the guy did his thing with Jake and Rodney's memories, which might end up even more fascinating than the dungeon.

The basement could wait for some other time.

"Stay here. They may need your help," he told his friends on his way out, then headed toward Kian.

Rooted to the same spot where Syssi had left him, Kian looked like the statue of *The Thinker*—except for the sitting part.

Poor jerk.

"How are you doing, big guy?" Andrew took a furtive glance at Kian's face, checking for fangs and glowing eyes. But it seemed Kian was holding it together, as evidenced by the absence of what Andrew had learned were the telling signs of an immortal male ready for battle—or losing his cool.

"Not one of my better days, that's for sure. Though I feel like a complete ass for saying that. I should feel relieved, grateful..." Frustrated, Kian raked a hand through his hair.

"You need sleep, buddy. You're exhausted. Everything that seems bleak now will look better after a good night's rest. Trust me." Andrew gave Kian's shoulder a light squeeze. "Are you in any shape to take care of my guys' memories? Or should they crash somewhere around here for tonight, and you'll do it tomorrow?"

"No, I'm fine. The sooner it's done, the better."

"Where do you want to do it?"

"I promised them I'd take them home and erase today's events before they fell asleep. To minimize the damage to their brains it's best to do it as soon as possible, and falling asleep right after will make it even better for them."

"I'm sure they'll understand if we change it a bit; make it easier for you."

"I'm not in the habit of breaking promises."

"You are in no shape to go driving around town after not sleeping for how long? Two whole days? Or is it three?"

"I appreciate your concern, but it is going to go down exactly as I've promised them."

"Okay, but on one condition—I'm driving."

"You got yourself a deal."

Once again, Kian surprised him. As stubborn and as obnoxious as he was, the guy wasn't above admitting weaknesses or accepting help.

A few minutes later, the gurney arrived, accompanied by a pretty petite redhead.

"Andrew, this is Bridget, our in-house physician," Kian introduced her. "Bridget, this is Andrew, Syssi's brother."

Andrew offered his hand and she took it, placing her tiny palm in his large one and giving it a short though surprisingly strong squeeze. "Welcome to our world, Andrew." The wide smile spreading across her face was as welcoming as her words. "We'll be seeing a lot of each other soon, I hope."

At first, Andrew assumed that she was coming on to him and reflexively straightened his shoulders and pulled in his abs. But then it occurred to him that it was highly unlikely—there was nothing flirtatious or coy in her demeanor.

Oh, right, she was referring to the transition.

Bummer.

"We'll see. I'm not sure about it, yet."

"No rush, take your time." She gave him a little pat on the arm and turned to go check on the prisoner.

The doctor had to wait a couple of moments as Jake and Rodney helped the brothers transport the unconscious guy out of the helicopter's cabin and onto the gurney.

She checked his vitals before letting the brothers wheel him away, then ambled up to Andrew.

Damn, he might have gotten it right the first time.

Bridget didn't bother to conceal the up and down look over she gave him. "Come and see me before you make up your mind. I'll give you a thorough check up to assess your general health. You'll want to know where you stand, health-wise, before deciding one way or the other."

"Sure will. Thank you."

This time, there was no doubt left in Andrew's mind that the pretty doctor wanted to get to know him better, and not strictly as a patient.

Hell, why not?

If things did not work out with Amanda, the

petite redhead was an interesting alternative. Bridget was not bad at all. Quite fetching, indeed.

Andrew smirked. Either one was a definite step up from his usual. Not that he had been in the habit of dating bimbos, but a professor? A medical doctor?

He would've never considered even approaching one—out of his league.

True.

But hey, this was before discovering he was a rare specimen, coveted by beautiful immortal females.

And as it turned out, he had a thing for doctors.

CHAPTER 2: AMANDA

hank the merciful Fates for Syssi, Amanda thought as she stood in Syssi's arms and sobbed her heart out. At least one person gave a damn about her and was happy to see her come home unharmed.

She'd really needed that hug.

Leaving Dalhu behind in the helicopter wasn't easy. But he'd been out throughout the ride, and just before landing Anandur had tranquilized him again. Fates only knew how long it would take Dalhu to shake it off.

And besides, with Kian out of the chopper, Dalhu was in no immediate danger.

Later, though? Amanda could only hope that Kian would leave Dalhu alone for tonight.

"I have a surprise for you," Syssi whispered in her

ear as she wrapped her arm around Amanda's waist and walked her toward the rooftop vestibule.

"I know, Andrew told me. I'm so happy for you!" Amanda pulled Syssi into another hug. It seemed as if she just couldn't get enough of those.

With Kian being a monumental jerk and giving her the cold shoulder, Syssi, with her concern and warm welcome, was treating Amanda more like family than Amanda's own brother.

Syssi punched the button for the elevator and glanced up at her. "How did Andrew…. oh, wait, you were talking about the transition?"

"Of course, silly, what did you think I was talking about?" Curiosity banishing her sad musings, Amanda ignored the ping preceding the quiet swish of the elevator doors opening.

"You'll see." Syssi pulled her inside. "The surprise is waiting for you in your apartment."

A moment later, as the doors slid open, Syssi pulled Amanda by the hand she was still holding, not letting go until they stood in front of Amanda's penthouse door. "Go ahead, open it…"

Arching a brow, Amanda turned the handle and slowly pushed open the door. Was there a Welcome Home banner hanging from the ceiling of her living room? Some balloons? Syssi was so sweet…

And what was that familiar, soothing scent?

It can't be…

"Ninni? Oh, sweet Fates, I can't believe it…" Amanda ran into her mother's open arms. The crack in the dam holding back the tears that had started in Syssi's arms became a gaping hole, and the waterworks resumed.

Amanda didn't know how long she'd cried. Vaguely, she remembered her mother pulling her to sit on the sofa and cradling her in her arms like a baby. But none of Annani's words had registered, only the effect of her soft, soothing voice.

When the last of the hiccups stopped, there was a mountain of used tissues on the floor, and a large margarita was sitting on the coffee table next to an oval platter of assorted cheeses and fruits.

One glance at the platter and Amanda started crying again.

"What is the matter, darling? You do not like the cheese? I can have Onidu take it away and replace it with another snack." Both her mother and Syssi regarded her with twin worried expressions on their faces.

"No, I like cheese, you know I do… It's just that Dalhu"—hiccup—"prepared a meal for me"—sniffle—"with cheeses and wine and fruit"—another sniffle.

"Oh, sweetheart, that does not sound so horrible. Did that Dalhu—I assume this is the name of your kidnapper—did he do something to hurt you after that meal? Is that why you are crying?"

"Noooo…" The *no* came out in a wail. But then after a few more sniffles and a hard blow into a tissue, Amanda dried her eyes and drained the margarita in two long gulps. She'd been babied enough. It was time to stop crying and behave like a grownup.

"He didn't do anything to hurt me. In fact, he was the most giving, the most attentive, the most accommodating male I have ever met. He treated me like a real princess, like I was precious, and certainly with more affection and respect than my own brother."

"I see." Annani nodded sagely.

Amanda braced herself for the lecture that was sure to follow. The one about how she wasn't thinking clearly and needed time to rest. Blah, blah, blah. "And don't think I'm suffering from Stockholm syndrome or some other psychological crap like that." Crossing her arms over her chest, she challenged her mother with a hard glare, then added a *humph* for emphasis.

"That is not what I was going to say. But I will not tolerate this kind of language or attitude in my presence. Uncross your arms, Amanda, you are not a toddler."

"I'm sorry. It's just that from the moment Kian saw me with Dalhu, he's been a jerk to me…" Amanda wasn't up for more rejection, especially not from her mother. It would destroy her completely.

14

But she wasn't sure how Annani would react to the news flash that her daughter had let a Doomer have sex with her. Not that they'd actually gotten that far. But Amanda wasn't going to pull a Clinton and claim oral sex didn't count.

"I think you should start from the beginning and tell us everything that happened. Unless you are tired and prefer to do it tomorrow." Annani took her hand and covered it with her other palm. "You are my daughter, Amanda, and I love you no matter what. There is nothing you can say that will change how I feel. Do not be afraid to share your burden with me. This is what mothers are for." She leaned up and kissed Amanda's cheek.

"You promise not to get mad?"

"I promise. But you look exhausted, and it can really wait for tomorrow."

"I'm beat, but I won't be able to sleep until I know… until I'm sure that you're not going to hate me for what I've done." Amanda sniffled and dropped her head onto her hands.

"Come, child, no need to be so dramatic. You can tell me everything."

"Okay." Amanda wrapped her fingers around the stem of the second margarita glass Onidu had handed her. "Thank you." She reclined into the comfort of the sofa cushions and crossed her legs.

"After leaving Syssi and her brother Andrew in

the restaurant, I headed to a jewelry store. My plan was to order a duplicate of the pendant Syssi gave me. You see, it was a present from Andrew for her sweet sixteen." She looked at her mother. "I didn't want her to get in trouble for giving it to me. But it must've been fated because that pendant is how they knew where to find me. Apparently, Andrew had a tracking device installed in it without Syssi's knowledge."

Amanda sighed and turned to Syssi. "He is so sweet. You are so lucky to have a brother who cares so much about you."

Syssi almost choked on her margarita. "Andrew? Sweet? Are we talking about the same guy?"

"Yes, he is a wonderful man. When Kian was treating me like dirt, Andrew was the one who asked me how I was holding up and offered his support."

"If you say so." Syssi chuckled.

"I know it was somewhat deceitful of Andrew not to tell you that he had a tracking device installed in the pendant. But he had only your best interest at heart. If it were you instead of me who was kidnapped, you would've been grateful to him for ensuring that you'd be found."

"Of course, I'm grateful. Realizing the tracker's significance, I even told Andrew he was my hero. Without it, we wouldn't have known where to even start looking for you."

"So that's that. You can think of him in any way you want, but to me, he is Andrew the sweet." Amanda shrugged. "But back to my story. So, I entered the store and immediately noticed a delicious scent, something male—enticing and calming at the same time—something that called to me like catnip to a cat. I looked around to see where it was coming from, and that was when I saw him—a gorgeous, huge male. It took only a moment for the clues to snap into place. He was an immortal, but not one of ours, therefore a Doomer. But that split second between realization dawning and my legs reacting to the command to move was more than enough for him. He pounced, his huge hand closing over my neck."

Amanda was getting into her story, enjoying the breathless anticipation of her small audience.

"I was terrified. I thought that he would tighten his grip and choke me at any moment. Instead, he bit me."

She paused to take another sip, her eyes darting between Syssi and her mother, who were scooting closer and closer to the edge of their seats with each new and exciting detail.

"It was incredible. I'd fantasized about an immortal male's bite for so long, but it was even better than I'd imagined My legs turned into two useless noodles, and I leaned into him. I'm embarrassed to admit it, but I wanted his hands all over me."

Amanda smiled sheepishly. "I even begged him to touch me. But he refused, saying he wouldn't do it without my sober consent. Can you imagine that? He said no to *me*..." She pointed at herself, regarding their shocked expressions with a satisfied smirk. "Then he took care of the girl at the counter, thralling her without even looking her in the eyes. Impressive, right?"

Her mother nodded. "Indeed."

"After switching cars with some guy at the mall, he took me to this motel and cuffed me to the bed. Normally, I could have just broken the wooden slats to get free, but I was loopy from the venom and so horny I was going out of my mind."

Syssi sputtered, spraying the coffee table. "Sorry." She choked. "I keep forgetting how nonchalant you people are about these things."

"It is okay, sweetie. No harm done," Annani reassured her with a pat on her knee. "Go on, Amanda."

"So, I was going out of my mind with lust... you okay, Syssi?" Amanda cast her a glance. The poor girl's cheeks were so red they must've been burning.

"Yeah, I'm fine. Go on," she croaked, touching the cool margarita glass to her hot face.

"I even cussed him out for refusing to provide the relief I needed. The guy was completely clueless about immortal females, but when he realized that I was really suffering, he gave me a sedative, saying he needed to retrieve stuff from wherever he and the other Doomers were staying. He must've done it while I was out because he was back when I woke up. I asked him what he wanted from me."

Syssi rolled her eyes. "Duh—"

"Yeah, that's what I thought. But it wasn't sex. Dalhu had something else in mind."

"He didn't want that? Is he gay?" Syssi interrupted.

"No, he is not gay. He said he wanted a future with me, wanted me for his wife, his mate, to have children with him."

"And what did you reply?" her mother probed gently.

"I told him he was delusional, of course. That there was no way to bridge the differences between us." Amanda sighed. If that were the only obstacle in their way, she wouldn't be sitting here with her mother and Syssi and telling a story instead of enjoying her man. "And not to forget the fact that we are each other's worst enemy." Though, that was no longer true... Dalhu had pledged himself to her.

"You know what his answer was?"

"What?" Syssi and Annani asked in unison.

"He said he would do everything to win my heart. Abandon the Brotherhood, support our cause, do whatever I demand from him. Except let me go, that is."

"Wow, that's…. well… kind of romantic… delusional, but romantic." Syssi squinted as if afraid her words wouldn't be well received.

"I know, right? But still, I asked him how he thought to achieve that impossible goal. He said we would run away and hide somewhere where we could spend some time together and get to know each other. I thought he was completely nuts. But what choice did I have? Right? He drove us to this remote cabin high up in the mountains, and on the way he broke into a store for provisions. But wait for it…" She paused dramatically. "He paid for it. Left cash on the counter to cover the cost."

The surprised expression on Annani's face should've been gratifying, but it wasn't. Amanda's dramatic delivery failed to give her the usual kick. Worse, it made her feel immature and foolish. But apparently, old habits die hard. Amanda wouldn't be herself without the added flourish. "I didn't realize it at the time, but this was the turning point. His behavior intrigued me. I began asking questions, and he told me about himself. He didn't try to make himself sound good and admitted that he had done a lot of killing during his long life. But I glimpsed something remarkable in between his words.

Despite all he had been through, there was still a small spark of light inside him. And honor."

"How old is he?" Annani asked.

"He is over eight hundred years old."

"For you guys, it's not that old," Syssi said.

"It is not young either. Go on, Amanda, I want to hear the rest of the story."

"We got to the cabin and, at least emotionally, it was a rollercoaster ride. There were moments I was terrified of him, and others when I was beginning to like him. Then for a little while, I was plotting to clobber him over the head with a shovel, but couldn't bring myself to do it because he was so incredibly nice to me. He even offered to send you a warning about the reinforcements his ex-bosses are sending to Los Angeles to hunt us down. Which reminds me that as much as I loathe to, I need to talk to Kian."

"What happened between Kian and you?" Annani asked.

"I'm getting there... Throughout our time together, Dalhu was doing exactly what he promised— everything he could to win my heart. And you know what? He was doing a damn good job of it. Obviously, it didn't hurt his efforts that he is so hot—very tall, beautifully built and sexy as hell—or the fact that my hormones went into overdrive whenever he got near me. I fought the attraction, but he was chipping away at the fragile wall of resistance I was struggling to keep up. Eventually, it crumbled last night, and I let Dalhu pleasure me. It wouldn't have ended at just that, but as I was coming down from the most fantastic completion I ever had, Kian blew a hole in the wall and leaped through it like some avenging demon."

"Oh, shit," Syssi blurted. "Sorry." She slanted a quick glance at Annani.

"No, 'oh shit' is appropriate in this case, Syssi." Annani got to her bare feet and began pacing. "I can guess what happened next, but please, continue."

"I must've screamed my head off when I climaxed, and Kian assumed I was being tortured."

Syssi snorted. "Sorry... I couldn't help it."

"And if my screaming wasn't enough to get Kian's blood boiling, I had Dalhu's shirt tied around my wrists... We were playing a game, you see..."

Amanda glanced sheepishly at Syssi and then at her mother. "Kian was already not thinking straight, so the moron didn't stop to think that a piece of fabric wasn't enough to restrain me for real. He attacked Dalhu, who was just defending himself while trying to protect me at the same time. It took me a moment to come down to earth, and as I did, Kian had his fangs embedded deep in Dalhu's throat and was about to tear it out."

Syssi gasped. "Oh, my god."

"I knew screaming at him would achieve nothing, not fast enough to save Dalhu, so I did the only thing I could. I tore out of the binding, jumped on Kian's back, and pulled at his head with all my strength while shouting and threatening him. Eventually, he let go. I tried to explain that the scream was one of pleasure, not pain, and that Dalhu didn't force me."

Recalling Kian's look of disgust, Amanda's gut twisted. She reached for her third margarita and drained it in one long gulp.

"You should have seen the way Kian looked at me," she whispered. "Like I was repulsive to him. Then, as if he couldn't stand the sight of me for even a moment longer, he issued a command to Anandur to cuff Dalhu and stormed out. He didn't say a word and hasn't looked at me since." Her chin began quivering, tears sliding down her cheeks.

Syssi moved to sit beside her and pulled her into a warm hug. "He'll get over it. You know he loves you."

"I'm not so sure. I gave him plenty of reasons to be mad at me before, but he never acted like this."

There was a long moment of silence, with her mother and Syssi deep in thought—no doubt trying to figure out a way to help her get back into Kian's good graces.

Yeah, good luck with that...

"The question is not if Kian would get over

Amanda's liaison with the Doomer. The real question is whether Amanda would. How do you feel about it, dear?" Her mother regarded her with her ancient, knowing eyes.

Right, that was the real question, and while her mind was still struggling with it, her gut already knew the answer.

But was she going to fess up?

Yeah, she was.

Amanda wasn't one to chicken out and had no intention of pretending she was going to let it go when, in fact, she wasn't.

"No, I'm not going to get over it. Not yet, and not because Kian disapproves. I do not claim to have fallen in love with Dalhu, but I certainly felt something."

Amanda trained her eyes on Annani as she continued in a near whisper. "There was this intimacy, a connection I've never experienced with a man before."

She humphed. "Heck, the only thing I ever felt toward a guy was lust, and the moment my needs were satisfied, I couldn't wait to be rid of him."

Amanda pushed to her feet, walked over to the bar, and poured herself another drink. "It might be as simple as immortal pheromones at work, or as complicated as a budding relationship, but I would like to have the opportunity to find out."

With the drink in hand, she sat back down. "But how? It's such a complicated mess. Kian has Dalhu locked up somewhere in the dungeon. And even though I believe Dalhu was sincere in his promises to me, I'm in no way suggesting we should let a Doomer, even an ex-Doomer, roam free. Or that we should embrace him with open arms and invite him to join the family. I'm not that naive." Amanda reclined into the sofa's soft cushions and closed her eyes.

She was so damn tired.

Her mother's small palm caressed her cheek. "Do not despair, child. It is a difficult situation, but not an impossible one."

Annani clasped Amanda's hands. "The three of us, working together, are powerful enough to conquer the world, right?" She waited for Amanda to nod. "Then unraveling this tangled knot should not be an obstacle too great for us to surmount. Do you agree?"

"Absolutely." Syssi stood up and joined Annani, placing her hand over hers. "Come on, Amanda. Put it here." They waited till she added her own hand to the pile.

"Thank you. Your support means the world to me." Amanda choked up. Her mother was right. Between the three of them, there was no way they wouldn't find a solution.

Annani pulled her hand out. "Although I'm sure both of you are eager, just as I am, to jump right in, our plans for world domination will have to wait for tomorrow. It is very late, and Amanda needs to recover from her ordeal." She winked and patted Syssi's hand, then gave Amanda's a tug. "Come, let us get you showered and then straight to bed."

Amanda didn't mind that Annani was pulling her by the hand like a small child, not at all, nor did she question why it felt so damn good to be ordered around by her tiny mother again.

"Good night, Syssi, whatever is left of it. We convene again tomorrow," Annani threw over her shoulder as she headed down the corridor to Amanda's bedroom.

"Good night," Syssi called after them, and a moment later Amanda heard her front door open quietly and close.

Syssi was such a good friend.

Maybe she could talk some sense into Kian. If anyone had a chance to break through his hateful attitude, it was Syssi. On the other hand, the girl was so timid, she might not be up to it. Syssi shied away from confrontations. Heck, she couldn't even bring herself to deal with David, who'd been tormenting her at work with rude, unwanted advances. It had gotten to the point where Syssi had been afraid to ask for his help with programming, even though she'd needed it desperately.

It might be a good idea to replace David with someone Syssi would be more comfortable working with. Professor Goodfellow wouldn't mind taking the guy off Amanda's hands. After all, though unpleasant, David was a decent programmer, and there weren't many available. Anyone with a knack for computers was working for tech companies and making double what the university offered.

Good idea. And while she was at it, she should hire more staff to work on her paranormal side project, or rather the main project as far as she was concerned. But for the university administration's sake, she still needed to maintain appearances and show worthwhile results on her official research. Luckily, she had her own financial backing and didn't need to explain a bloated staff to anyone.

Now that her hypothesis about Dormants displaying paranormal abilities had been proven right, Amanda wanted to run with it, not walk.

Tomorrow, she would talk with Syssi and together they would plan a course of action to put the search for Dormants on a faster track.

CHAPTER 3: DALHU

*D*alhu woke up in a dark, dingy prison cell, or so he thought. But as he raised his arm to check the time on his watch, a harsh, blinding light flooded the place.

What the hell? Bloody motion detectors?

After a couple of seconds, his pupils adjusted to the bright illumination, and he swept a quick look around, taking stock of his surroundings. The windowless room was tiny, about seven feet wide by ten feet long, and bare—save for the mattress under him. At the back, a utilitarian bathroom area extended the space by another five feet or so and was separated from the main room by a low privacy wall made of semitransparent glass blocks.

Pretty standard for a single occupancy jail cell. Except for the door, which was a monster. The thing was at least twelve inches thick, and he knew this because there was a little glass door at the bottom of it and then another one about a foot away.

So he was in solitary confinement, and they planned to provide his meals through that contraption. Smart.

Still, he'd expected worse.

Hell, these accommodations were luxurious compared to some of the places he'd stayed in. And not as a prisoner. The room was clean, free of mildew, and the mattress didn't stink. There was a clean sheet over it, and they even provided him with a warm blanket.

Both smelled new.

Other than that, there were the requisite cameras, mounted high up on the ceiling where even he, as tall as he was, couldn't reach them.

Real clever. There was nothing he could fashion a weapon from, and no real privacy.

He was going to lose his fucking mind in no time.

The situation reminded him of a scene from a silly movie he had once seen, *Rocketman*, if Dalhu remembered correctly. As part of his training for a space mission, the would-be astronaut was locked for twenty-four hours in a container about the size of this room. Passing the time singing nonstop and enacting puppet shows with his socks, he drove his competitor in the adjoining tank insane.

Maybe Dalhu could do the same. Trouble was, he didn't know any songs, and he wasn't wearing any socks.

Great, his only entertainment option was thinking about his impending torture and execution.

Or worse, torture and indefinite imprisonment.

With a muffled sigh, Dalhu got up and went to check out the facilities. Finding a new toothbrush and a battery-operated shaver inside the niche over the sink was a pleasant surprise. There was no mirror, but then he didn't need one to use either. He brushed, shaved, and showered, then got dressed, putting on his old clothes.

When he got back to the room, the first thing he noticed was the tray of food in the compartment behind the little glass door, and he took it out. Sitting on the mattress, he placed the tray on the floor in front of him. Again, he was pleasantly surprised—the coffee was excellent and the two sandwiches were loaded with cold cuts. A decent meal.

Who knew, maybe this was the worst his rich captors could dish out. He doubted anyone had taken pity on him or had cared to treat him kindly.

Unless this was meant to be his last meal. Though, if this were indeed the case, they should've at least served him a juicy steak. And a stiff drink.

Did he dare entertain hope that it had been Amanda's doing?

Nah. He knew her better than that. She would not have bothered with food. If anything, she would've been on the other side of this door, demanding to see him.

Yeah, as if there was a chance in hell she cared for him—enough to defy her brother.

Dalhu wondered whether she would visit him, at least one last time to say goodbye, or forget all about him and let him rot in here alone.

After all, she'd never claimed to have any feelings for him. And engaging in sexual activity was as meaningless for her as it used to be for him...

With her, though, it had been nothing but. More like a life-altering experience. He'd been different with Amanda, and not just in the way he'd interacted with her, but on a more visceral level...

He felt as if he'd been reborn in that cabin, reshaped to become the man she needed him to be.

Still, it might have been all one-sided.

True, she'd defended him against her own brother. But there was a big difference between not wanting to see him dead and wanting to be with him.

Yeah.

It was time to wake up from the dream and face his grim reality. He needed to get back to the way he'd been before. Ruthless and cold would get him through this, romantic and soft would not. After sorting out his new cache of feelings and memories, he would lock it away inside the minuscule compartment dedicated to the good he'd experienced throughout his life.

Dalhu finished the last of the coffee and returned the tray to where he had found it, then went back to sit on the mattress.

With his back slumped against the wall and his elbows crossed over his up-drawn knees, Dalhu buried his face in his arms and delved into his cache of precious memories.

For a long time, it had been the memory of his mother and sister that had kept him from losing it and surrendering to the darkness around him.

The sound of his sister's giggles, the image of his mother's indulgent, loving smile—those memories had sustained him during other bleak times, and he'd desperately clung to them for decades. But inevitably, they were doomed to fade.

Amanda had gifted him with new ones.

He'd had so little time with her, and there had been precious few of them. But he cherished each and every one.

Aside from what he'd experienced with Amanda, and what was left of what he'd once had with his family, there was nothing else in his life worth remembering.

Hell, he would've paid good money to forget most of the crap he'd been through.

This new cache would have to sustain him for shit knew how long. Provided he escaped execution. But just in case he got to live, he wanted to preserve every little detail of his time with Amanda.

CHAPTER 4: ANDREW

s he drove back to the high rise, Andrew barely managed to keep his eyes open, let alone concentrate on the road. And it didn't help that neither he nor Kian was in the mood to chat.

First, they'd dropped off Jake at his home and then Rodney. Despite being exhausted to the point of nearly passing out, Kian had insisted on waiting for each to shower and get in bed before doing his thing with their heads.

Just as he'd promised.

"You'd better crash at my place and get a few hours of sleep before heading home," Kian offered as they reached the underground parking.

For a moment, Andrew was tempted to play it tough and pretend he was perfectly fine to drive back to his place. But that would've been stupid.

And pointless.

In his youth, when impressing his friends had been paramount—safety and self-preservation a far-flung, distant notion—he would've said he was okay. He would've driven home even if it meant forcing his eyelids open with his fingers the entire time. But those days were long gone, as were the days when he could've pushed it, going without sleep for two or three full cycles while still functioning at close to optimal level.

He was getting old, and as much as he hated to admit it, particularly to himself, he could no longer pull the same shit he had been able to—with ease—a decade ago.

And wasn't that a bitch.

A midlife crisis before forty.

Reluctantly, he nodded, eased into an empty spot, and cut the ignition.

They made the trip up to the penthouse in silence. Kian unlocked his front door and headed down the hallway to his bedroom, just pointing to one of the doors he had passed to show Andrew where to crash.

The guy was operating on fumes. The difference was that it had taken Kian three days without shut-eye to reach this state. Andrew, on the other hand, had had a full night's sleep less than twenty-four hours ago.

It wasn't a good feeling—relatively young, but already over the hill—at least for any kind of active field duty, that is. Of course, he could still supervise, train, plan missions, spy—do all the things that required his knowledge and experience, but not physical strength, agility, and endurance.

It sucked balls.

Taking a perfunctory, one-minute shower, he got into bed naked and slid between the sheets. In his own home, it was standard operating procedure. As a guest? Yeah, not so much. But he didn't have a change of clothes and asking Kian to borrow some of his was not cool.

Most likely, the guy was already sleeping. And if he wasn't? Well, then he was probably busy doing other things… with Syssi…

Yeah… no need to go there.

Exhaustion taking over, Andrew's eyelids slid shut. But as soon as they did, the image of Amanda's naked perfection popped behind his closed lids, and he grew instantly hard.

Shit, his damn erection didn't give a rat's ass about the rest of his body not being on board for the wakey-wakey.

Reaching under the covers and fisting the bad boy, Andrew felt like a dirty old man. Though come on, occasionally, every guy whacked off to the image of a woman he wasn't involved with—even those who fronted the holier-than-thou attitude. The only men who didn't, couldn't, or took a turn at the self-serve station to the image of another guy.

Andrew chuckled. If Amanda were a famous star, her poster would be hanging over every teenager's bed, providing the boys with inspiration for endless hours of self-play.

Funny thing was, he had the distinct impression that she wouldn't mind. In fact, he was pretty sure she would love it.

What a woman.

Stroking himself, he pictured Amanda in all her naked glory.

She was magnificent, standing in the middle of that cabin with her hands on her hips and her foot tapping the floor, staring Kian down while ignoring the rest of her drooling audience. Hell, the woman couldn't have looked more confident if she were addressing a courtroom dressed to the nines in a power suit.

Having every detail of her stunning face and perfect body already memorized, Andrew tried to go a step further and imagine himself with her. But the face of that Doomer intruded on his fantasy, turning the hard club in his hand into a limp noodle.

He tried again, focusing only on Amanda, but it was no use.

Andrew sighed and turned on his side. It was

probably nothing. The bad boy down-under had evidently gotten a bitching memo from management about him draining the last of the energy reserves and had finally agreed it was time to give it a rest.

It wasn't like the guy was malfunctioning or anything. He had never let Andrew down before. And there was no way in hell Andrew was accepting any other explanation.

CHAPTER 5: KIAN

*O*n his way to the bathroom, Kian glanced at his empty bed, regarding it with mixed feelings. He would've loved nothing better than to snuggle up to Syssi's warm body and have her lovely scent soothe his raw nerves. But it was good that she was with Amanda.

At a time when he couldn't even bring himself to look at his sister, let alone provide comfort, Kian was grateful to Syssi for being there for her. Not that he would've been capable of doing much good under normal circumstances—providing a shoulder to cry on wasn't his style. He was more of a kick to the butt kind of guy.

Amanda needed someone to unload her ordeal on—someone who cared for her and would listen and *ah* and *huh* at all the right places without passing judgment. True, their mother was with her as well, but Kian wasn't sure if Annani was any better at handling an emotional crisis than he was.

From his experience, it depended on his mother's mood. At times, she had been supportive and understanding, but more often than not she'd expected him to toughen up instead of seeking solace from her. But maybe Annani was more indulgent toward Amanda. After all, no one expected the princess to assume a leadership position, which would have demanded a steel backbone of her. Unlike Sari and Kian, the princess was allowed some slack, and Annani might be more inclined to grant her some motherly comfort.

Still, there was no one better for the job than his sweet, empathetic Syssi.

During the long drive to Jake's place in Valencia, Kian had plenty of time to think, and it had helped clear his head. Not that he had a choice. He had to force himself to calm down in order to do a decent job of suppressing the guy's memories without damaging his brain. Later, after they had left Rodney at his home in Santa Clarita, Kian had done more soul searching on the drive back home.

As he'd sifted through their memories, watching the replay of what had happened over at the cabin and seeing himself through their eyes hadn't been easy. It had been a chilling eye-opener. And even though they had only seen the tail end of his attack, from the mortals' perspective he'd looked like an out-of-control madman raging at a traumatized, vulnerable, naked woman.

An incredibly beautiful, naked woman.

It had been no big surprise to witness the males' reaction to Amanda in her birthday suit, but he hadn't expected the almost worshipful reverence they had been hit with. The poor schmucks had been literally rendered stupid.

No wonder they'd immediately taken her side.

Nevertheless, as much as he would've liked to, he couldn't entirely dismiss Andrew's buddies' opinion as biased, or their assessment as inaccurate—regardless of the back story they had been missing.

Still, to be able to see things in a different light, he needed to let go of the rage.

Easier said than done, though. And in Kian's case —impossible.

His deep-seated hatred for his enemies was built upon two millennia of witnessing their unimaginable cruelty and their complete disregard for human life.

True, the atrocities had been executed by the mortals under the Doomers' control. But to say it had been the mortals' fault was like blaming the finger for pulling the trigger and not the brain commanding it. But to be perfectly honest, he couldn't blame the Doomers for all of it. He was well aware that some of the *humans* hadn't needed any outside influence.

There were always those who thirsted for the rush of power they got from the killing and the raping and the terror and destruction they wreaked. In the past, bloodthirsty thugs had joined armies; nowadays, they joined terror organizations and *rebel* groups. The motive was the same, though—to indulge their evil appetites with impunity.

But when people who would've otherwise spent their entire lives without committing even one act of cruelty became monsters, there was influence behind it.

Some called it the Devil. Kian had another name for it—The Brotherhood of the Devout Order of Mortdh—The Doomers.

It wasn't a case of a different ideology, or a fierce competition between rivals, or even a personal vendetta. This was a battle over the fate of humanity. Kian and his clan wanted it to thrive; the Doomers wanted it to yield to their power.

And to that end, the Doomers were doing everything in their power to keep the human population divided, ignorant, and fearful.

So yeah, Kian felt well justified in his hatred. But be that as it may, he shouldn't have extended it to his own sister, despite her momentary lapse of judgment—even if it had been a monumental one.

In fact, the sex with her captor had probably been Amanda's way of coping with a terrifying situation, and convincing herself that she wanted it had made it tolerable.

But even though the shift in logic helped him see things in a different light, Kian still felt contaminated by the filth that had soiled Amanda.

Standing under the spray of the almost scalding water, he kept running the soap over his body, over and over, wishing he had one of those loofah things to better scrub with. In the recesses of his mind, Kian was aware that the stain he was trying to rub off was on the inside, but he couldn't help the compulsion.

His only consolation was that Syssi wasn't there to witness his slip into insanity.

CHAPTER 6: AMANDA

"Where is he?" Amanda rounded on Anandur the moment his door cracked open.

The racket she'd made pounding on his door should've been enough to rouse the whole floor, and yet the guy had taken his sweet time getting his butt in gear.

Through the sliver of an opening, Anandur peeked at her with a tight-lipped stare. Then, after a long moment, he swung it open and turned back inside, flashing her his naked ass. She followed, waiting impatiently as she heard him flush the toilet and brush his teeth, then watched him plod to his bedroom to finally emerge wearing a pair of unbuttoned jeans.

Without sparing her a glance, Anandur

continued to the kitchen and got busy making coffee.

Insufferable man.

Were all the males in her family jerks?

At last, as the coffeemaker spewed its few remaining drops, filling the two cups he'd shoved under it to the brim, Anandur pulled one for himself and handed her the other. "Milk is in the fridge, but I would check the date if I were you. Sugar is right over there." He pointed to the cluttered counter.

Amanda humphed in indignation but accepted the mug. After all, coffee was coffee and she needed her fix. After a horrible nightmare had awakened her way too early, she'd bolted up from bed, barely pausing to pull on a T-shirt and a pair of jeans, let alone stop for coffee.

Terror clawing through her, she'd grabbed her phone and texted Syssi.

Thank heavens, her friend had answered immediately. Syssi had reassured her that Kian had been sleeping soundly beside her. And that no, the clothes he had worn before coming to bed hadn't been bloodied.

Amanda had made Syssi check.

With panic shortening out her brain, it had been a miracle that the idea to ask Syssi had managed to surface from that disjointed swirl.

Even now, knowing it had been only a dream,

the image of Dalhu's mangled body had her heart hammer a drumroll against her ribs. Hanging from chains bolted to a stone wall high above him, he'd been so beaten and bloodied that she'd barely recognized him. His manacled wrists had been broken, and his ankles had been secured by links bolted to the floor, his feet pointing in the wrong direction.

Amanda shivered. She hadn't needed to see the face of his tormentor to know it had been Kian. She'd heard his voice, distorted, demonic, while he'd tortured Dalhu for information, demanding more and more...

Except, Dalhu had had no more to give. He'd already told Kian everything.

Rationally, Amanda accepted that it hadn't been real, but she needed to see Dalhu with her own eyes to banish the last vestiges of that nightmare.

That being said, though, she could spare a few moments to drink her morning coffee.

The milk turned out to be fine, and she poured some into her cup, then added sugar. "Okay, enough stalling. Tell me where you dumped Dalhu. I want to see him."

Leaning against the counter and sipping his hot brew, Anandur just stared at her for a long moment before responding. "He is down in the dungeon. It's on the same level as the rest of the *guest rooms*, but in a section that is better secured and not as lavishly appointed."

"Take me to him."

"I can't, not without Kian's authorization. And frankly? Hell would freeze over before he allows it."

"Then we'll go over his head."

"What do you mean over his head? Kian is at the top of our food chain."

"Wrong. My mother is. Or did you forget that she is still the head of our clan? The fact that she lets Kian and Sari run things as they see fit and doesn't interfere with the day to day operations doesn't mean she can't or wouldn't. After all, we are not a democracy, and she has the final word."

"You've got a point there. You'll have to forgive me, though, if I demand to hear it from her own lips... or in writing. As it is, I'm in enough trouble with Kian already over that little incident with Syssi."

"Damn you, Anandur. Since when did you turn into a wuss? My mother is still sleeping, and I really need to see Dalhu now. I had this horrible nightmare about Kian torturing him. It was so bad that I didn't even brush my teeth before rushing down here."

Anandur arched a brow, but then his face softened. "You can rest easy. No one tortured your Doomer. Kian left with Andrew and his men, going straight from the helipad to the garage. And I'm sure

47

he was too exhausted to torture anyone when he came back. But if you need to see your Doomer so badly, I have a solution that can ease your mind without getting me in trouble or waking a sleeping goddess and risking her wrath."

"Yeah? What is it?"

"We can go down to security and view him on the surveillance monitors."

"Anandur, you're a genius. Let's go." Amanda put her empty mug on the counter and reached up to kiss his cheek.

"I'll be damned, wonders never cease. First Kian, and now you? Two compliments in less than twenty-four hours." He shook his head as he headed for the bedroom. "I wish Brundar was here to hear it. He would never believe me."

"Why? Where is he?"

"Who knows?" Anandur answered from the bedroom. "He is a secretive bastard."

That was true. Brundar was the most tight-lipped guy she had ever met.

Anandur came out of the bedroom tugging on a T-shirt. "Let's go, princess. Your frog awaits."

"Does he do it a lot? Stay the night somewhere else, that is?" she asked as they entered the elevator. Amanda couldn't help her curiosity. Brundar was such an enigma that every morsel of information about him, no matter how small, was a rare treat.

"From time to time. Not often, though. I've learned not to ask because I never get an answer." Anandur crossed his arms over his chest and leaned against the elevator's panel.

"Care to hazard a guess?" Anandur had to know something. Not only was he Brundar's brother, but the two worked and lived together.

Anandur shrugged. "I assume it's sex. When we go clubbing, he doesn't go for the females, and I know he doesn't use paid services either, not any that I'm aware of, anyway. But he has to get it somewhere, right?"

The elevator stopped on the second floor and Amanda followed Anandur out. "Do you think he is gay?" she whispered.

"No, I know he isn't. His reaction to females is the same as any other heterosexual, horny immortal male's."

"So what do you think he's hiding?" she asked as they reached a set of gray double doors that were secured with a card-reader lock.

"I don't know. But if Brundar wants to keep his sex life private, it's his prerogative. Right?" Anandur slid his card through the scanner and pushed the left door open.

Amanda had never seen the place before, and as it turned out, Security was not what she had imagined. Instead of one room full of monitors and a guy watching them with a bored expression on his face, the Security Department was huge, occupying most of the second floor's office space and employing dozens of people—mortal and immortal.

Lording supreme over the whole thing was the gatekeeper—Rose the receptionist—a formidable elderly human.

She smiled at Anandur while Amanda got the tight-lipped who-is-that-floozy look-over. "I'm sorry. But Dr. Dokani doesn't have the necessary clearance. You'll have to go in by yourself, dear," Rose rasped in her smoker's voice.

It took some of Anandur's famous charm, or maybe it was the veiled threat of a possible retribution from the big boss that did the trick, but eventually the harpy relented and buzzed them in.

As they made their way down the long hallway, Anandur poked his head into the various rooms and explained their function. Besides several viewing rooms that were each in charge of monitoring a different section of the building, there was also a weapons room, the head of security's room, a changing room with rows of lockers, and even a small staff cafeteria that doubled as a rec room.

Greeting everyone by name, Anandur introduced Amanda as his *cousin*.

For some reason, the appreciative looks she got from the guys failed to thrill her—annoying her instead—and she was glad to reach the end of the tour.

Anandur swiped his access card to the only room in the security wing that was restricted to immortal personnel only. Not that the humans were aware of who their coworkers were, of course. As far as they were concerned, the restricted access only meant that a higher clearance was required.

Over there, surveillance tracked the floors occupied by the clan, including the private underground garage, the rooftop, and the entrances to the dedicated elevators. Though, if needed, they had access to all the other camera feeds as well.

Two guys and one girl were working the twelve-hour night shift, which would probably be over soon. Early dawn had been on the horizon when she'd left her apartment.

"Hi, Steve, how're you, buddy?" Anandur slapped hands with the guy. "How is our lone prisoner doing?"

"Sleeping, I think. Here, these are the two feeds from his room."

Amanda waited for the monitors to come online, but when nothing happened she got impatient. "Well? How long does it take to turn them on?"

"They are on. It's just dark in there. That's why I said he was probably sleeping."

Dark? Pitch black was more like it. If even she,

with her enhanced eyesight, could see nothing, then there was absolutely no light in the room.

"Has he woken up at all since we brought him in?" Anandur placed a hand on Amanda's shoulder, halting the rant that was building up.

"Yeah, he did. Got up, used the bathroom, ate breakfast, then went back to sit on the mattress. But after five minutes of him pulling the Rodin, sitting motionless, the sensors turned the lights off. That was a little over an hour ago."

"Could you rewind the footage? Amanda wants to make sure he is okay."

Steve gave her a quizzical glance, then shrugged and did as Anandur had asked, starting the recording from the moment the brothers had brought the unconscious Dalhu into the room and had transferred him from the gurney to the mattress.

The room—if one could call it that, more like a closet—wasn't as bad as in her dream. The walls were painted a plain cream color, and there were no chains or even hooks to attach them to in sight. But other than that, it was shockingly small and bare.

A few minutes after the guys left and locked the door, the lights switched off, and the monitors went black.

"Speed it up," Anandur said.

Steve did just that, and once Dalhu woke up and

the lights switched back on, he slowed the thing to only four times the normal speed.

As she watched Dalhu in the video while they fast forwarded, it was obvious he'd been aware of the cameras, and as his gaze had swept over every detail in the room, his expression had been guarded, revealing next to nothing. But Amanda knew him well enough to notice the little tell signs he had been working so hard to conceal.

He looked hopeless.

Not that she could blame him. Being locked in a small inescapable box, with no hope of ever getting out, who wouldn't feel despondent?

But he was wrong.

Dalhu underestimated what she could and would do for him, and more importantly, who she had in her corner.

When the recording ended, and the monitors returned to live feed, the little number at the top left corner of the screen showed it to be a little before seven in the morning. It was still too early, considering that Annani had gone to bed less than two hours ago. Nevertheless, she was going to risk rousing her mother.

"Thank you, Steve. Let's go, Anandur."

"I'm having Dalhu moved," she said once they were out of the security wing and back inside the elevator.

"You know I can't do it. Kian selected this cell specifically. That's where he wants him to stay."

"I know. I'm going to wake my mother."

"Oh, boy, the shit's gonna hit the fan."

Amanda glanced up at Anandur with a half-hearted smile. He was right. This was going to get real nasty, real fast. And for once, she wasn't looking forward to all the drama.

"Good luck," Anandur said as they reached his floor. "I'm going back to sleep. Don't wake me up unless an all-out war is raging."

She smiled. "Good night, or rather good morning."

He nodded, giving her the thumbs-up as the elevator doors were about to close.

Back in the penthouse, Amanda paced around her living room for a good ten or fifteen minutes. Before waking her mother, she needed to work on phrasing her request to sound as convincing and as respectful as possible.

Despite what she'd told Anandur, she wasn't certain at all Annani would agree to go over Kian's head. In fact, she was pretty sure her mother would take a lot of convincing.

True, Annani had promised her support, but her mother's idea of helping was probably talking with Kian and attempting to reason with him.

There was no doubt in Amanda's mind that her

mother would balk at undermining Kian's authority over his own keep.

Shit. Amanda didn't like it either.

She had to find a way to have Dalhu transferred to a decent room without an all-out battle with Kian.

CHAPTER 7: DALHU

The darkness didn't bother Dalhu, nor did the quiet. The lack of outside stimuli provided a blank canvas for his imagination. He filled the void with images of Amanda, painting them in vivid colors on the inside of his eyelids, and the silence with her voice, playing her spoken words like a soundtrack in his head.

He was committing to memory each and every nuance of her expressive face, her perfect body. The smiles. The way she tapped her foot on the floor when angry. The arch of her perfect dark brows when doubtful.

Her spirit.

She was such a passionate woman, and he wasn't referring to sex. Although, yeah... that too. She was just as enthusiastic about her work—finding a solution to her clan's plight.

Fuck. As Dalhu's head jerked up, activating the motion detectors, the harsh light flooded his cell again. Amanda would not be able to return to her work. Not as long as the men he had foolishly left behind—alive—knew who she was, where she worked, and what her face looked like.

Even if she were to change her name and establish a new research laboratory elsewhere, they'd still be able to find her.

As long as they lived, Amanda would never be safe.

Damn. He hadn't planned for the contingency of her ever going home, and therefore had never considered what would happen if she were to be rescued.

Amanda would want to return to her work at the lab as soon as possible.

He'd been careless. He'd fucked up and had failed to protect Amanda again. What the hell had he been thinking? What had possessed him to spare their lives? He should have eliminated each and every last thread leading to her.

I'm such a fucking idiot.

Dalhu pushed up from the mattress and began pacing. Like a caged animal, he walked in circles around his tiny jail cell, struggling to suppress the roar that was building up in his chest.

Up until that moment, he'd been careful to project a strong image for the benefit of the guys watching him on the surveillance cameras, refusing to give them the satisfaction of seeing him lose it.

Not anymore.

Lacing his fingers behind his head and pressing the heels of his palms into his temples, he didn't give a shit if his captors were watching.

Let them see his distress.

Let them gloat.

He had to talk to Amanda and warn her.

But how? How would he communicate with her?

The fuckers watching the monitors wouldn't tell her if he asked for her, and anyway, it wasn't likely that they were monitoring sound in addition to visual in this rattrap. If the room were ever to be used for interrogation, it would have been rigged with audio recording equipment. But Dalhu doubted a cell this size could accommodate such activity. Besides, there was no residual scent of blood. And it wasn't like prisoners in solitary confinement were known to talk to themselves and reveal secrets that were worth recording.

He had the passing thought that if he were to trash the place, someone would come to check on him. Except, there wasn't much to trash, and the room was probably soundproof. No one in the adjoining cells or the corridor would be able to hear him; only the guys in security would know anything was going on.

In the end, desperation drove him to employ a last-resort measure. He turned his face up to the camera and began miming.

From a warrior to a fucking mime.

How low the mighty had fallen.

Doing the chatting thing with his lips and the fingers of one hand, he pointed to his head with the other. Hopefully, the guards were better at charades than he was, and weren't mistaking his gestures to mean he was hearing voices in his head.

Asking to talk to someone in charge, Dalhu mouthed the words and gesticulated with his hands. Repeating his request, he even tried to shape his hands into something resembling a crown on his head.

Damn, he could only imagine the ridicule his performance was garnering.

"*N*inni?" Amanda whispered and dipped her head to kiss her mother's warm cheek. "Are you awake?" she whispered again.

It was dark in Annani's bedroom. The closed shutters blocked all outside light from filtering through, and the room would have been pitch black if not for the lambent glow cast by the Goddess's luminous skin.

"No," Annani rasped, a small smile blooming on her delicate face. "I am still sleeping and dreaming my little Mindy is afraid of the dark and wants to crawl in bed with her Ninni. Come, child, get in and let me hug you." She lifted the comforter and scooched back a little, making room for Amanda.

Hesitating for all of two seconds, Amanda hopped in and snuggled up to her mother. And if anyone had a problem with a two-hundred-year-old woman wanting a little babying from her Ninni, they could shove it where the sun doesn't shine.

Annani let the comforter drop back, then lifted her palm to Amanda's cheek and cupped it gently. "What troubles you so early in the morning?"

"I had a bad dream."

Annani chuckled and shifted up, kissing Amanda's forehead. "Here, I kissed the bad dream away. All better?"

"You know what? It's funny, but it is."

"Of course it is. Love always brightens the mood."

Amanda sighed and moved to lie on her back. "I had a horrible nightmare. I dreamt that Dalhu had been tortured. It was so awful that I woke up with my heart up in my throat, and I just had to check on him to reassure myself that he was okay. But knowing Kian would never allow it, I tried to get Anandur to take me to see Dalhu. But Anandur refused to go over Kian's head and took me to security instead. I watched the recording from the surveillance cameras, all of it, from the moment they'd brought Dalhu in and up to that moment. As far as I could ascertain, he wasn't harmed. But his cell is tiny, with nothing but a mattress on the floor. He is a big guy, taller even than Anandur, he'll go crazy in there."

Amanda paused and sighed again, adding a soft

sniffle for effect. "I don't know what to do, Ninni. I'm well aware that we can't risk letting a Doomer roam free about the keep, and I'm not suggesting it. But I can't stand the thought of Dalhu being locked up in that little empty box. Besides, I want to be able to visit him and spend some time with him without everyone in security watching and listening to everything that's going on. You know what I mean?"

She sniffled again, a little louder this time. "Talking with Kian will achieve nothing. In fact, the opposite is probably true. If I try to reason with him, he'll just get angrier and may take it out on Dalhu." As real tears slid down her temples, trickling into the crease between her shoulder and neck, Amanda covered her eyes with the palms of her hands.

Annani's reply was a long time in coming. "Do not worry, child, I will talk to him."

"Kian won't listen to reason, not even from you."

"Oh, but my dear Mindy, you underestimate me. By the time I am done with Kian, he will be convinced it was his own idea to move Dalhu to a better holding room."

"How? Are you going to use influence on him?"

It was a disconcerting thought. As far as Amanda knew, Annani had never used her power to manipulate her own children, but what if she had? As the only one capable of playing with the minds of immortals, she could've done so with no one any the wiser.

Except, why would she?

Whenever Annani wanted something from her children, or from any of the other members of her clan for that matter, all she had to do was ask. No one would dare defy her. And it wasn't as if the Goddess shied away from voicing her demands.

"No, of course not," Annani humphed. "I will simply do what every other mother does... well, maybe not every mother... just those with a flair for the dramatic." She winked. "I am, after all, a diva, and my loving son is obligated to cater to my whims, however bizarre."

Amanda smiled at her mother's wink. "What do you have in mind?"

"Patience, my dear, you will see."

CHAPTER 9: ANANDUR

"*W*hat?" Anandur barked into his cell phone. What the hell could Steve want less than an hour after he and Amanda had left the control room? Interrupting Anandur's sleep for the second time this morning?

He'd only just managed to close his eyes when the incessant ringing forced him to answer the damn thing. "Steve, buddy," Anandur hissed, "unless we are under attack or there is a raging inferno in the building, I don't want to hear about it. I'm going back to sleep."

"Sorry, bro, I hate to do this to you, but it was you or Kian, and I chose the lesser of two evils. Our prisoner is trying to communicate... Excuse me for a moment," he said as rolling laughter sounded in the background. "Shut up, you morons!" Steve's admonition was muffled, indicating that his hand was covering the receiver. "Sorry about that, the idiots think it's funny—" He snickered. "I'm so sorry, it's just that the Doomer doesn't know we can hear him, and he's been miming for the past half an hour that he needs to talk to someone in charge. The poor bastard is getting more and more creative with each new charade." Steve snorted, then inhaled deeply to calm himself. "I think you should check what his problem is. He says it's a matter of life and death... Unless you want me to call Kian..."

"No, damn it, don't call him. I'll handle this."

"I thought so."

"Fucking Doomer," Anandur muttered under his breath as he threw off the covers and pulled on the jeans he'd dropped on the nightstand before getting back in bed. In the bathroom, he splashed his face with cold water and brushed his teeth, again. Looking up, he groaned. Not that he needed the damn mirror to show him that he looked like hell— with the color of his bloodshot eyes matching the color of his hair.

Damn, he'd better get some sleep before hitting the clubs tonight, or he'd scare the ladies away.

Nah, not going to happen.

Nothing short of his demonic illusion could keep females from lusting after him. Anandur flexed his impressive pectorals and smirked. They could never resist all of this.

Yeah, even with eyes that were red-rimmed and underlined by dark circles he was still one hell of a handsome devil. Getting closer to the mirror, he patted a few wayward curls in place. His beard needed a trim and so did his mustache, but it would have to wait. His barber was off today, and Anandur didn't trust himself with the task. It was too damn hard to manage the dense bush.

Shaving it off, however, was not an option. Without it his damn baby face, though pretty, looked too young. Absurd, considering the fact that he was over a thousand years old. Problem was, even though he loved an eyeful of young flesh as much as the next guy, he preferred to bed women, not girls. But experienced, older females preferred men in their thirties, not twenties, which was what he looked like without the beard.

This was the only concession he made, though. With his height and muscular build, it was more than enough. Anandur bought his clothes wherever he could find stuff his size and paid no attention to fashion trends or designer names. In fact, he liked shopping at discount stores even though he could afford better things. That way he knew for sure that the ladies were after his body and not his wallet. Besides, it was easier to just grab something at

Walmart than get hassled by the sales people working at the fancier places.

Grabbing the T-shirt he'd left on the bathroom floor, he brought it up to his nose for a sniff. It was still fresh. After all, he'd put it on only this morning when Amanda had so rudely interrupted his sleep. Nevertheless, he tossed it into the hamper and headed back to his bedroom for a new one.

A male could never be too fastidious about his personal hygiene, especially body odor. The more virile the male, the more potent the stench, hence the more grooming required.

Not that Anandur's obsession with cleanliness extended to his and Brundar's apartment. The place would've looked like a pigsty if not for Okidu showing himself in, every couple of nights or so, to tidy up.

Pulling a plain, gray T-shirt over his chest, Anandur headed to Brundar's room. If he was lucky, his brother was back, and he would send him down to deal with the Doomer. Not that it was likely, but he could hope.

Nope, Brundar wasn't back yet.

Crap.

Anandur made himself a big mug of coffee, strapped a dagger to his calf, pocketed a wicked switchblade, and headed for the dungeon while cursing his good-for-nothing brother and the damn Doomer all through the elevator ride.

Besides the Doomer, the *guest* level had no other occupants at the moment. After his transition, Michael had moved in with Kri. And Kian had released Carol, who up until last night had been chilling in the same miserable cell they had thrown their new *guest* in.

Used for solitary confinement, it was the nastiest they had.

The poor girl had been begging pitifully to be released, promising she would never ever get drunk in a bar and yap so irresponsibly again. Kian would've probably kept her there for another twenty-four hours, but he'd needed the room and had called Onegus from the chopper to let her out.

When he reached the end of the corridor, Anandur stopped in front of the Doomer's room and punched in the code, engaging the mechanism to open the cell's heavy steel door. As the thing started its smooth, but slow swing-out motion, he rested his other hand on the switchblade in his pocket. Not that he expected any trouble from the Doomer, the guy seemed smarter than that. But as the saying went, better safe than sorry, or the other one about not trusting a scorpion or something like that.

As soon as the door fully opened, the Doomer

backed away and raised his hands, palms facing out, to show he wasn't planning anything.

Anandur stepped in. "So, what is so urgent that I had to drag myself out of bed and come down here to look at your sorry face?" And a sorry face it was, the haunted look in the Doomer's eyes leaching out the bite from Anandur's tone.

"Thank you for coming. I would invite you to sit down, but as you can see, there is nowhere to sit. Unless you want to join me on the mattress."

"Sorry, dude, but you're not my type." Anandur heaved himself up on the half wall that delineated the bathroom area. "Okay, talk, I'm listening."

The Doomer didn't sit either. Instead, he leaned his back against the wall and crossed his arms over his chest.

"Are you in charge here? Or is it the other guy? Kian, Amanda's brother?"

Obviously, the Doomer had no clue who either Amanda or Kian was, or he wouldn't be asking who was in charge.

Smart girl, she didn't tell him.

"I'm all that you are going to get, so talk."

The Doomer regarded him for a split second longer, then dipped his head. "I made a mistake." He looked up. "When I ran with Amanda, I decided not to eliminate the men under my command. I thought it would look less suspicious to those in charge if only I went missing, not the entire team. I even left my men with the impression that I was going after a Guardian, so when I didn't return, they would assume I was taken out. That way, I thought, no one from my side would come looking for me. But now, because of my unforgivable miscalculation, Amanda is in danger. They know who she is and where she works."

His expression was blank, a guarded mask as he delivered his request. "You need to take my men out before the reinforcements arrive, and before they can share what they know with the others."

"Are you serious? You want us to kill your men?"

"Yes."

"Cold bastard, aren't you?" Anandur pinned him with a hard stare.

The man didn't flinch, his expression stony as he locked eyes with Anandur. "I am, but that's beside the point. These men are mindless cogs in Navuh's machine of destruction, and they are deemed disposable even by their own people. If given the chance, they will come after you and your family and relish killing your men and raping your women. So if I were you, I would not shed a tear at their demise."

"I definitely wouldn't. I'm just surprised at the nonchalant way you are offering me their heads on a platter."

"I don't give a damn who I have to off to keep her safe. Or to put it bluntly, other than Amanda, I just don't give a damn about anyone."

Shaking his head, Anandur chuckled. "I have to admit, it's kind of romantic. Gruesome, but heartfelt."

Dalhu's expression didn't change as he appraised Anandur. "What would you have done in my place? If you were lucky enough to find a woman who meant everything to you, was there anything you wouldn't have done to keep her safe?"

Yeah, probably not, with the exception of sacrificing his family.

Well, that wasn't precisely true. Some members of his clan he wouldn't mind.

Still, he understood where the guy was coming from. Having an immortal female to form a lifelong bond with was every immortal male's dream, with maybe the exception of those who were gay. Not that the Doomer had a chance in hell of achieving it. But Anandur could sympathize with the guy's yearnings, delusional as they were.

Even if he weren't a coldhearted bastard, the Doomer had nothing and no one to care for. The Brotherhood of the Devout Order Of Mortdh wasn't exactly a nurturing organization.

No wonder the guy had no qualms about offing his brethren for Amanda's sake.

"Kian, your mother is on the phone." Syssi ran a gentle palm up and down Kian's bicep.

He cracked one eye open and yawned. "What does she want?" Did it only feel like he'd gone to bed a few minutes ago? "What time is it?"

Holding her thumb over the phone's mic, Syssi whispered, "It's fifteen after eight. She says it's important."

What the hell could Annani want that couldn't wait until later? As in much later? After he had his fill of shut-eye and of Syssi? Or maybe the other way around...

Even in his exhausted state, Syssi's innocent touch had stirred him. But it wasn't as if he could refuse the call and have Syssi tell Annani to call later.

Stifling a groan, he reluctantly accepted the receiver from Syssi. "What is it, Mother?" Kian tried and failed to hide his irritation.

"I am sorry to disturb your much-needed slumber, Kian. But it is imperative that I talk to your prisoner as soon as possible. You can take care of it for me in less than a minute, without even leaving your bed. Just instruct Anandur to arrange the meeting and then go back to sleep."

It took a moment for her words to penetrate his sleep-addled brain. "What? Why the hell would you want to do that?" He jerked up to a sitting position and gripped the receiver, hard, easing up only when the plastic began to bend.

"I will forgive your slip, Kian, but only this one time," she said imperiously. "Anandur has just visited with the prisoner. The Doomer insists there is some sort of danger we need to address immediately before it is too late. I need to hear what he has to say."

With a sigh, Kian swung his legs over the edge of the bed. "I'll do it. I don't want you anywhere near that... that thing, Mother." There were some other choice adjectives he had in mind, but heeding her warning about language, he stopped himself in time.

"I understand your concern for my safety, my sweet boy. But I am in no danger, as you well know, and I wish to talk to the prisoner. It is a rare opportunity to have some of my questions about the Brotherhood answered and to learn about Navuh's future plans. I am not asking your permission, Kian. All I need is for you to make the arrangements."

Damn it. When Annani made up her mind, it was futile to try to reason with her. And it certainly sounded like she wouldn't budge on this one.

"I see that I have no choice, but I'm coming with you."

"Please do not. I have no need of a chaperone. Anandur will suffice as my protection. And you, Kian, need your sleep. You are no good to anyone when you are grumpy and snappy because you are exhausted."

This wasn't good. In Annani speak, she was telling him she didn't want him to be there, and there was nothing he could say or do to convince her otherwise.

But that didn't mean he couldn't take every precaution he could think of. She was right, of course. The Doomer, however big and strong, posed no real danger to her. She could immobilize him with one mental command. Nevertheless, imagining his tiny, delicate mother in the same room with that monster went against every protective instinct in him.

"Give me half an hour."

"Thank you. I will be awaiting your call."

With a groan, Kian heaved his legs back onto the bed and dropped his head against the headboard, then reached for the mug of fresh coffee Syssi was holding for him. "You're a life saver. Thank you."

"So, what's going on? What did she want?" Syssi sat on the bed and snuggled up to him, placing her palm over his bare chest.

He took a sip and cleared his throat. "She wants to talk to the Doomer."

"Is it a problem? You think he'll try something?"

"Not likely. Nevertheless, before I allow her in the same room with him, I'm going to make damn sure he's neutralized."

Syssi smirked as she stroked his chest, playing with the few hairs she found there. "I don't think your mother would appreciate seeing Dalhu chained to the wall. Or drugged. Her idea of interrogation is probably a pleasant chat over drinks and hors d'oeuvres."

"I know. This is exactly what I'm trying to figure out. How the hell am I going to secure a room in a way that will not offend her sensibilities? And without being too obvious about it?" Kian rubbed his brows.

Syssi leaned and planted a small kiss on his chest. "I'm sure you'll figure something out. Just be quick about it so you can go back to sleep and recharge." She extended her little pink tongue and licked at his nipple. "There are some promises"—lick—"you've made"—another swipe of her tongue—"that I'm still waiting for you to fulfill," she said, her voice husky.

He was tired, but not that tired.

Syssi squeaked as he pulled her up to lie on top of him, and tried to wiggle away. He captured her neck, holding her still and kissing her deep and slow.

She moaned, rubbing herself all over his erection.

"You just wait until I'm done taking care of this thing for my mother... then I'm going to take care of you."

"Not until you've gotten several hours of sound sleep." Once again, she tried to wiggle out of his arms.

Kian tightened his hold and in one swift move flipped Syssi, pinning her underneath him. "I don't think so," he growled, pressing down and letting her feel how hard she had gotten him.

She gasped, and her eyelids fluttered, her body softening in surrender.

"My sweet Syssi." He eased his hold and kissed her gently, then nuzzled at her neck, inhaling the intoxicating aroma of her arousal. "I love you," he whispered into her skin.

It was incredible, the way she made all his troubles seem trivial. With her thighs cradling him in a loving embrace, he gazed at her flushed, beautiful face and felt at peace with the world.

Unfortunately, the world was demanding his attention, and although he was tempted to tell it to go to hell and then make love to his woman, he couldn't.

Instead, he took one more quick kiss and rolled off her. "How about you stay here and wait for me?" he said as he got up and headed for the bathroom.

Syssi scrambled to get out of bed. "You need to sleep. And I can see that it's not going to happen as long as I'm here."

She was absolutely right. If he got back in bed and she was still there, sleep would be the furthest thing from his mind. He would pleasure her as he had promised until she screamed loud enough to…

"That reminds me," he called from the bathroom. "If you haven't noticed, Andrew stayed over and is sleeping in one of the spare bedrooms."

"The way he snores? I think everybody in the keep knows he is here. He sounds like a broken blender." Syssi leaned against the door frame and watched Kian as he brushed his teeth, eating up his naked body with hungry eyes.

With a grin, Kian flexed a little.

Her breath hitched. She licked her lips.

Sweet.

"Like what you see?" he taunted, using a small

washcloth to dry off the water drops from his face and chest—slowly.

"Oh, you're a wicked, wicked man. I'm going to the kitchen." She pushed away from the frame and left, the door swinging closed behind her.

Pity, he wanted to tease her for a little longer.

CHAPTER 11: AMANDA

"*H*i, Anandur, what's up?" Amanda glanced at Annani and clicked her phone's speaker button on.

"I don't know how you managed to pull it off, but Kian just called. He wants me to transfer your frog into the largest *guest room* and secure it for Annani's visit."

Yes! Amanda gave her mother the thumbs-up. "I had nothing to do with it. Kian must've realized on his own that Dalhu's tiny cell is inappropriate for any kind of visit, let alone Annani's. You know Kian, he would've never allowed her to be cooped up with a dangerous Doomer in such small quarters." She did her best to sound nonchalant. After all, the whole point of this maneuver was about preserving appearances and not challenging Kian's authority or undermining his status as the leader of this keep.

"Yeah, right… have it your way. Oh, and get a hold of this, he asked me to lend the Doomer some of my clothes. Kian wants him to look presentable for her highness."

Looking at her mother with new appreciation, Amanda grinned. Everything worked like a charm. "You don't say… that's a good idea. And don't worry, I'll pay you back for the clothes."

"No need, princess. But I would take an IOU for a future favor."

"You got it. What should I tell Annani?"

"I'm on my way down to the dungeon. As soon as I'm done there, I'll come up and escort her to the prisoner. It seems she refused Kian's offer to do the honors, which by the way, he sounded quite peeved about. He wants me to stay glued to her side at all times."

"I'll tell her to be ready. See you later." Amanda terminated the call and turned to give her mother a hug.

"You did it, Ninni."

Annani's smug face had 'I told you so' written all over it. "I'm glad Anandur, and not Kian, will come to escort me down to the dungeon. I was not sure about Kian's compliance with this part of my request. "

"You mean, us," Amanda corrected.

"No, child, I am going to see the prisoner by myself. You can visit him after I come back."

"But why? Anandur is going to be there, and probably other Guardians as well," Amanda whined.

"Your presence there will distract Dalhu. I want his full and undivided attention, and I do not want him choosing his words carefully and omitting things on your account."

For a moment, Amanda considered producing a little sniffle or two to soften her mother's resolve. But as one drama queen to another, she suspected her antics wouldn't work on Annani.

And besides, she could use the time to choose an outfit and make herself pretty.

The tough part was to decide what look she was going for. Elegant and refined? Sexy? Casual?

What did she want to achieve on her first visit?

Sex, of course, was foremost on her mind. After the little taste Dalhu had given her at the cabin, she couldn't wait to finish what had been so harshly interrupted.

The memory of the incomparable pleasure he'd wrought out of her was still so fresh, she felt her breasts grow heavy and her core spasm with need.

Amanda shivered.

She had the nagging suspicion that mortals just wouldn't do anymore.

After having been exposed to the exquisite taste of such rare wine, going back to the *meh* variety would be a serious letdown. Better go without than compromise for something subpar.

Trouble was, the rare wine came from a forbidden fruit.

It would have been so much easier if she had been able to forget all about Dalhu and give Andrew a chance. Andrew and Kian seemed to get along fabulously, and everyone else would welcome Syssi's brother into the family with open arms.

Heck, maybe she would. Fates knew the whole thing with Dalhu was tenuous.

Andrew was a great guy, and what's more, he obviously still wanted her, even after that talk they had on the way to the chopper, during which she'd made sure that he had no illusions as to the sort of woman he was pining for. He knew who and what she was. Except there was always the chance that, like most guys, Andrew had been blindsided by her beauty, but she didn't think so. Andrew wasn't the impressionable type.

Dalhu, on the other hand, believed Amanda could walk on water. And that was while he was still clueless about who she really was. Though not for long. After the chat he was going to have with her mother, the cat would be out of the bag. And heavens only knew how he'd react to that.

He might resent her for keeping this information from him, and there was the distinct possibility that he would be intimidated by her status.

Or, he might react the way she hoped he would, telling her that there was nothing that could change the way he felt about her.

Amanda chuckled. Dalhu had no idea how apt he'd been when he'd called her *princess,* or how much this *Princess Buttercup* liked having her own *as-you-wish* guy.

She sighed. Sex would have to wait.

They needed to talk.

CHAPTER 12: DALHU

*D*own at his cell, Dalhu tensed as the whiz of the pneumatic bolts retracting preceded the slow swing-out motion of his cell's door.

How heavy was that thing that an immortal male couldn't swing it open manually? Or were they just too spoiled to exert themselves by pushing it?

Figures, with all that money...

"It's your lucky day, frog." The redheaded Guardian walked in with a small bundle of clothes under his arm.

"Frog?"

Was this some new kind of insult he wasn't familiar with?

"You know, like in the princess and the frog

story. The princess kisses a frog, and he turns into a prince. Though in your case, you're no prince, just a garden variety frog." Anandur handed him the small bundle. "Here, I brought you some fresh clothes."

"Why?" Dalhu was genuinely perplexed. The clothes Anandur was handing him didn't look like prison garb, and even though his captors were rich, it didn't mean that they were obliged to provide their enemies with anything more than the bare necessities. And it wasn't as if he was offending their sensibilities by wearing dirty or torn stuff. Hell, Dalhu was better dressed than the Guardian. The plain gray T-shirt the guy was wearing looked like something he had paid five bucks for at a discount store.

"Because I'm just nice like that." Anandur winked. "Go change, I'm moving you to a better room."

"Not that I don't appreciate the kindness, but I'm suspicious of what you would want in return." He regarded the redhead warily. The guy didn't strike him as gay, but maybe he was just very good at fronting a hetero. After all, not all gay men flamboyantly overdramatized femininity. Though, in Anandur's case, the Guardian would have to be a superb actor to project such a powerful masculine, heterosexual vibe.

Anandur snorted. "As I've said before, you're not

my type. Get over it, dude, and go change. I promise not to peek." He winked again, this time licking his lips in an obvious leer.

The guy must be just messing with me... or is he?

Going behind the privacy wall, Dalhu hesitated before taking his clothes off. But a quick glance at the Guardian reassured him he had nothing to worry about. The guy was leaning against the wall and watching something on his phone.

Still, better to be quick about it.

Taking a one minute turn in the shower, Dalhu washed again. Not that he felt dirty, but he hated the idea of changing into fresh clothes without washing first.

"You're oddly fastidious, for a Doomer," Anandur commented as Dalhu came out dressed in the new, or rather used clothes.

Surprisingly, they fit, though barely, and he suspected that their original owner was the redhead. Anandur was almost the same size as Dalhu, maybe an inch or two shorter, but he was bulkier, probably outweighing Dalhu by a dozen pounds or so.

"You've got a problem with that?" Dalhu was used to taunts about what the other guys considered as his excessive bathing habits.

"No, not at all, to the contrary. It is just that I find it unusual for you guys." Anandur opened the door, and they stepped out into the wide corridor. "The others I had the displeasure of getting acquainted with stank to high heavens." The Guardian grimaced. "I hate stinkers," he grated, stopping in front of another door and punching a code into the panel.

Inside, two males, Guardians by the look of them, were seated at a round dining table, busy playing a card game. There was also a sofa and two armchairs as well as a flat-screen TV. No bed, though. But there was another door, maybe leading to a separate bedroom?

They gave him a suite?

What the hell was going on?

"These are my comrades, Bhathian and Arwel." Anandur made the introduction. The men nodded and went back to their game.

Evidently, there was no need to introduce Dalhu.

He turned to his unlikely new friend. Granted, referring to Anandur as a friend was a stretch, but at least the Guardian wasn't openly hostile and treated Dalhu decently. "Please, tell me what's going on? And why am I suddenly treated like royalty?"

"You're not, but your visitor is."

"What visitor?"

"And what? Spoil the surprise? No way."

Dalhu's heart skipped a beat. Was it Amanda? Was she coming to see him?

Except, why call her royalty...

Anandur had called her princess, but Dalhu had assumed the guy meant it as a form of endearment, same way he had. If not for the lavish suite and the additional guards, he would've dismissed the whole thing as Anandur's peculiar sense of humor. But now he wondered. Was Amanda someone important? Aside from the importance of her research, that is?

"Enough with the fish-out-of-water thing. Go plant your butt on that sofa. Do not get up or make any sudden movements until after your guest leaves. Am I clear?" Anandur was all business now, all traces of humor gone.

Dalhu didn't get the fish-out-of-water reference, but he had no problem understanding the rest. Anandur and the two other Guardians were there to ensure the mysterious guest's safety, and if Dalhu even twitched the wrong way, they were going to jump on him.

For the life of him, though, he couldn't understand why they didn't just put him in chains. Better yet, strap an electric collar around his throat and zap him if he made a suspicious move.

In their shoes, this was what he would've done.

The Guardians didn't carry any visible weapons either. They must be very confident in their hand-to-hand to forgo those while guarding him.

Not that he doubted their abilities. He had been at the receiving end of the Guardians' fighting skills time and again. Not personally, but they had proven their superiority over the men he had sent against them.

"I'm leaving you in the capable hands of my colleagues. Don't give them any trouble while I'm gone." Anandur pointed a finger at Dalhu and pulled open the door.

Dalhu nodded, and Anandur stepped out, closing it behind him.

Dalhu heard the whiz of the lock engaging. The door to this room was nothing like the monster securing his previous lodging, but he wasn't fooled by its slender profile. It was probably reinforced with thin titanium rods, which locked into a door-jamb that was probably enhanced as well. The Guardians were not stupid. They wouldn't put him in a room he could break out of.

Unless, this was only a temporary reprieve, and he would be returned to that tiny cell after his mysterious rendezvous was over.

Shortly after Anandur left him under the watchful eyes of the two Guardians, a stout, weird-looking butler brought in a tray of assorted appe-tizers and placed it on the coffee table in front of Dalhu.

The two Guardians eyed the thing with interest but refrained from sampling.

The butler walked up to the double door cabinet behind the dining area and opened it, revealing a well-stocked bar. He pulled out a carafe, filled it with some dark liquid from the fridge, and together with two crystal goblets brought it over to the coffee table.

The one named Arwel got up from his seat, leaving his cards face down on the table, and stepped up to the bar. He poured himself a drink.

"You want something?" he asked the other one.

"No. I don't drink before lunch," the surly one bit out.

Arwel shrugged. "Suit yourself." He sat down with his large drink in hand and picked up his cards.

No one thought to ask Dalhu. Not that he would've accepted. He didn't drink before lunch either. And anyway, it was imperative for him to stay sharp for the audience with his guest—whoever he might be. *Or she... hopefully, she...*

"Yeah. It's all good... No, nothing at all," Arwel said, though it didn't look like he was addressing Bhathian. The tone and the small pause indicated that he was talking to someone outside the room, and a quick glance confirmed the almost invisible earpiece hiding under the guy's hair.

Dalhu tensed. Watching the door, he squared his

shoulders and forced his hands to stay loose on top of his knees—palms down.

He heard the mechanized buzz and then the click of the lock a moment before the door swung open.

Anandur stepped in and nodded his head once, approving of Dalhu's obedient pose, before stepping aside to let the *important guest* in.

Looking up, Dalhu almost missed the first clue, but following Anandur's eyes, he glanced down and saw a dainty foot cross the doorjamb, followed by a tiny red-haired female in a long black dress.

She turned her face to him, and time stopped, then exploded like a bolt of lightning.

Later, when he'd think back to this moment, he'd remember that it felt like being shocked by a mighty bolt of electric power, but sans the pain, only the glory.

Forgetting Anandur's warning, Dalhu did what he was compelled to. He dropped to his knees and prostrated himself before the Goddess.

"It's okay. He's just awestruck." He dimly heard Arwel stopping Bhathian from lunging forward.

Awestruck could not begin to describe it.

She was the real thing—a real Goddess—and she was magnificent.

For some reason, whenever he thought of Annani, he imagined a female version of Navuh. A tall, dark, majestic woman, with an angry scowl permanently etched on her handsome face.

The real Annani was so far beyond whatever a mortal or an immortal could conjure in his imagination.

She was otherworldly.

Awesome power, indescribable beauty…

And love…

Dalhu felt guilt crushing down on him like an anvil—couldn't fathom how he could've ever hated this… this Goddess?

For the first time in his life, he understood the meaning of the word sacrilege. As one who had never believed in a higher power, he had sneered at those who were offended by what they perceived as disrespect for their deity.

But if he had known the real Annani, he would've been more than offended. He would've been outraged by any negative comment about her. And to think he'd been guilty of much worse? That he'd harbored hate in his heart for a goddess that was the material representation of love and beauty and all that was good?

"Oh, my dear boy, there is no need for that. Please rise." Her voice sounded like heavenly chimes.

More than anything, Dalhu wanted to obey, but he was frozen in place.

"Come on, frog. Up you go." Anandur's amused

voice managed to break the spell, and Dalhu lifted to his knees.

The Goddess was so small that from his kneeling position he was almost eye to eye with her. He caught a glimpse of her smile before lowering his eyes.

"It is permitted to gaze upon my face, and you do not need to kneel either. Make yourself comfortable on the sofa. I wish to converse with you." She gave him a little pat on the top of his head.

Awkwardly, he pushed back to sit without standing first, afraid his towering height would somehow be offensive to her. Never mind that Anandur wasn't that much shorter than him. But then again, Anandur wasn't a hated enemy either.

As the Goddess gracefully lowered herself into one of the armchairs, from behind her Anandur pointed a finger at Dalhu in warning, then moved to join his friends at the card table.

"Lift your head and let me see you," she commanded.

He did, taking a furtive look at her impossible face, childlike and yet ancient.

She regarded him in silence, her smart eyes appraising. "I understand now what my daughter sees in you. You are very handsome, strong."

Daughter? Like a real daughter? Or did the Goddess refer to all of her progeny as her children?

She must've read his mind. "Yes, Dalhu, Amanda is my daughter." She smirked. "The youngest child of my womb," she clarified.

Struck by lightning, again.

Speechless.

Hopeless.

The little hope he had harbored that Amanda would somehow find a way for them to be together had just been pulverized.

"Do not look so despondent, Dalhu. Where there is a will, there is a way." She winked.

Annani, the only Goddess known to exist, had actually winked at him.

"Now, tell me more about the danger to my daughter."

Dalhu dropped his head. Choosing his words carefully, he swallowed and cleared his throat. "My men know that Amanda is an immortal and that she works at the university. It wouldn't have been an issue if she'd remained in hiding. With me—"

He swallowed again, his eyes flickering over to the Goddess's face. Her expression remained impassive.

"Now that she is back home, Amanda will want to resume her work. I know how important this research is to her... to all of you." Dalhu glanced at the Goddess again.

She nodded.

"Time is of the essence. Reinforcements are arriving shortly, and once they do, containing this will become impossible. We have a small window of opportunity to eliminate the threat."

"They might have already surrendered the information," she countered.

"I didn't inform my superiors about Amanda, and the men's low ranking prohibits them from calling headquarters directly. Besides, they will do nothing without being ordered to do so. They'll wait for me to come back or for my replacement to arrive."

"Are you sure about that?"

"Positive."

"Well, in that case, we definitely need to make our move quickly. However, I am not keen on using the extreme measures you suggest."

"Every member of the Brotherhood you get rid of is one less threat to you and your clan. If this were my family—and despite your opinion of me, I consider Amanda and by extension all of you as such —I would do everything I could to keep it safe."

In the background, he heard the snorts and *humph*s his proclamation had elicited, but he ignored the Guardians, focusing on the Goddess instead.

Annani was difficult to read, but he had a feeling she approved. And hers was the only opinion that mattered.

Still, minutes passed as she mulled it over before

she spoke again. "I wonder. Is it common in the Brotherhood? This every-man-for-himself attitude? And I mean no offense by it, but I wonder how such an organization functions without its members being loyal to each other." She tilted her head a little, the mass of her big, red curls sliding over one delicate shoulder.

Dalhu lifted his hand to rub at his mouth, but then hastily dropped it back to his knee, heeding Anandur's warning. Besides, who knew what the Goddess considered as good manners, and avoiding unnecessary hand movements seemed like a safe bet. "No, it's not common. However, the chief loyalty of the simple soldiers is to the cause and to Navuh. Their own lives and those of their comrades are deemed inconsequential, and they are more than happy to make the ultimate sacrifice on the altar of the holy war," he bit out.

Out of respect for the Goddess, Dalhu suppressed the anger bubbling to the surface. How many years of his life had he spent being just as stupid as the others? Believing in a ridiculous cause that had nothing but hate and envy at its roots? A cause that preached destruction and death as an ultimate goal?

"For a long time, I've been just as blind and dumb as they are, but eventually, I figured it out. Navuh's agenda is the same as any other power-hungry despot's—world domination. And the only way he knows how to achieve it is to ensure that humanity is plagued by wars, ignorance, and superstition, therefore easy to manipulate. Are there others like me? I must assume I'm not the only sharp tool in the shed, but it is not like we could seek each other out and form a club. Unless it's the severed heads club," he chuckled.

Annani didn't smile at his clever pun. If anything, she looked saddened. "It is hard to overcome the relentless brainwashing, nay impossible. I am glad that you were able to break free of it, Dalhu, but I doubt there are more than a handful of males like you, if at all." She sighed. "I wish there were another way. After all, my clan and these immortal males are all that is left of our people."

Dalhu had no clever answer to that. It surprised him, though, that she still thought of members of the Brotherhood as *her people*.

Yes, they'd originated from the same seed, but they'd branched in opposite directions. Besides their unique genetics, they had nothing in common— polar opposites, black and white, good and evil.

It was as simple as that.

Not that he was going to correct the Goddess, but she was blindsided by her own goodness, mistakenly believing that there must be some good deep down in the hearts of her enemies.

There was none.

Breaking free of the brainwashing didn't mean Dalhu had miraculously become good. He was still as dark and as evil as he had been before.

His love for Amanda was the only good he had in him.

CHAPTER 13: AMANDA

"So, how did it go?" Amanda pounced on Annani as soon as Anandur brought her mother back. The *little chat* had taken much longer than she had expected.

Her mother had been gone for over an hour.

With a sad little smile, Annani cupped Amanda's cheek. "Let us go out to the terrace." She let her arm drop and glided out through the open sliding doors.

Amanda's gut twisted. What was that melancholy look all about?

"I'll be back later to take you down to your frog," Anandur threw over his shoulder as he headed out. "Half an hour tops."

"It's okay. Take your time," she called after him. Right now, hearing all about her mother's conversation with Dalhu took precedence over seeing him.

Joining Annani on the terrace, Amanda drew out a chair and sat across from her mother at the round bistro table. "Well?"

"He is handsome, that is for sure. Tall and strong." Annani paused to wave Onidu over. "Could you please serve us some Perrier, Onidu?"

Amanda waited till the butler left. "And?" She crossed her arms and began tapping her fingers on her biceps.

"I know you want to hear that I approve of Dalhu. But based on only one conversation, I cannot. Not wholeheartedly."

Amanda's spirit sunk. "No, of course not," she mumbled.

"He seems really taken with you, and I believe him when he says he would do anything and everything to ensure your safety. But…"

Oh boy, here it comes. Amanda held her breath.

"He is obsessed with you. For him, the sun and the moon revolve around you. You may think it is a good thing, but it is not. This kind of passion forms an unhealthy attachment, one that has the potential of turning deadly. That being said, though, I have to consider that Dalhu's abnormal fixation on you might be temporary. He is desperate and sees you as his only lifeline. It is also reasonable that his worry for your safety is keeping him on edge." Annani accepted the glass of soda from Onidu and took a little sip.

"I don't understand. What are you trying to say?"

"I am saying that you should be careful. Go ahead and visit with him, indulge a little..." Annani winked. "But guard your heart, and do not tell him any more than he already knows."

Amanda snorted. "Yeah, right, as if I'm going to do anything in front of the surveillance cameras and provide the guys in security with homemade porn."

Her eyes sparkling, Annani smiled a mischievous little smile and leaned forward to whisper, "Anandur is taking care of it for you. There would be no camera feed from the bedroom, just the living room." With a smug expression on her beautiful face, her mother leaned back in her chair.

"How did you get him to agree to that?"

With a barely noticeable grimace, Annani shifted in her chair. "He agreed on the condition that he is going to be there with you, guarding."

Amanda's brows shot up. "Really?"

"You can close your mouth, Amanda. He is not going to be in the bedroom with you. He is going to wait in the living room." Annani made it sound like it was a nonissue.

"But he is going to hear everything! How am I supposed to even get in the mood with him eavesdropping? And you know Anandur, he will have a field day with this. The man is the worst kind of gossip."

Amanda was not shy about her sexual endeavors, but she balked at having an audience.

Annani looked hurt. Probably because Amanda wasn't as ecstatic over this arrangement as she had expected. "He promised he would keep your forays into the bedroom secret. And you should know that one does not make promises to me in vain. Besides, it is in Anandur's best interest that Kian never finds out about it. This was the best I could do. It was not easy to persuade Anandur to join in on our little conspiracy. You know how I hate bending my own grandchildren's will to my own. I'd rather they cooperate out of love and respect. Luckily for you, it appears that our Anandur is a romantic at heart."

Oh, hell. This was just peachy.

Why couldn't it have been someone else?

She would've been more comfortable with stoic Brundar on guard duty, or any of the other Guardians for that matter. Anandur was the least respectful of the bunch, and the fact that he had promised not to reveal her secret didn't mean he wouldn't use it to torment her mercilessly.

On the other hand, she was pretty sure none of the others would've agreed to cooperate, fearing Kian.

Admittedly, Annani had chosen their coconspirator wisely. Anandur was the only one brazen enough to risk Kian's wrath.

She'd take it. After all, beggars couldn't be choosers.

"Thank you." Amanda took her mother's small hand and gave it a gentle squeeze.

"You are welcome."

"So, what else did you talk about? You've been gone for an awfully long time."

Annani lifted her hand to her chest. "Oh dear, you would not believe the things he has told me."

"What? Is it about the danger he was talking about?"

"Among other things, but that wasn't the worst of it. Though, if you were ever to fall into their hands it definitely would have been the worst." Annani shivered. After a moment, she leaned and lifted the carafe, pouring herself more sparkling water.

Her mother wasn't a woman easily shaken, but she seemed distraught over what she had learned. After several long sips, Annani placed the glass back on the table and squared her shoulders, regaining her regal composure. "First, about the immediate danger to you. I do not know if Dalhu told you, but he was the leader of a small unit of Doomers. The men he left behind are aware of who you are and where you work. Not that you are my daughter, of course, but that you are an immortal. For now, he is adamant that his men will not do anything without being ordered, and that this knowledge is contained. But with reinforcements arriving shortly, your identity will become known throughout their organization. All the way to the top. You will be forced to remain in hiding indefinitely. No more teaching, and no more research. Not unless you conduct it in a private facility and erase your test subjects' memories as soon as you are done with them."

That would be a disaster. Amanda loved teaching and loved her lab. She even liked hanging out with the other professors. Not because any of them were hot, but because she enjoyed having an intelligent conversation with well-educated, smart people. "What does he suggest we do?"

"Eliminate them. He gave us the address of where his six remaining men are staying. We have already taken care of five out of the eleven he started with. He believes we killed them."

"Didn't we?"

"No, I forbade it. They are entombed in our crypt."

"Why? And how did you get Kian to agree to spare them?"

"I had to order him to do it. I knew he could never be persuaded. He would have never agreed. And as to why? I cannot bear the thought of destroying what is left of our kind. Even Doomers. Maybe one day, if the merciful Fates smile kindly upon us, their leader will somehow be eliminated and their organization will disperse. I cling to the hope that the effects will eventually fade without the relentless brainwashing."

"And then you will wake the sleepers?"

"Yes."

Amanda snorted. "An immortal version of the end-of-days prophecy."

Annani tilted her head and lifted her palms. "What can I say? I am an optimist, and I'd rather avoid the irreversible when there is a viable alternative."

"So, are we going to kill Dalhu's men... sorry... entomb them? I guess they are as good as dead while entombed, so why not. Less guilt is always good. Right?"

"I have another idea I want to run by Kian first."

"What is it?"

"You will have to wait. I need to think it through before I talk it over with Kian."

"Fair enough."

Sinking back in her chair, Amanda tilted her face up toward the morning sun. She welcomed the warmth.

Dalhu's cold disregard for the lives of his men shouldn't have surprised her. After all, he had told her as much himself. Still, it was a chilling reminder that the accommodating, romantic male she'd been with was a recent creation—a thin veneer of bright paint over scars that ran deep and long.

Scars that no amount of care and time could heal.

CHAPTER 14: AMANDA

ith all the hard questions buzzing around in Amanda's head, and no clear answers, by the time Anandur returned to escort her down to the dungeon, her stomach was churning, and she felt nauseated.

A quandary wasn't something Amanda experienced often. Most issues, she didn't care enough to give a damn about, and when addressing those that actually mattered to her, she found it easy to reach a decisive conclusion based on relevant information or even pure gut instinct.

Not this time, though.

During the ride down to the basement, she avoided Anandur's eyes, not ready to deal with the condescending smirk she was sure to find there. Instead, she checked herself in the elevator's mirror.

Adjusting the collar of her silk blouse, Amanda regarded the conservative outfit she had chosen— one of her modest teacher getups. She looked good, of course, but not hot...well, relatively speaking... not hot by her own standards, but still...

In a way, her choice of outfit reflected her contemplative rather than lustful mood.

"Why so somber?" Anandur punched the dungeon's floor number. "I thought you'd be happier about finally seeing your frog. And by the way, you owe me, big time. If Kian ever finds out, he is going to go ballistic on my ass." For a change, Anandur wasn't joking. The big guy looked worried.

"I appreciate it. But if it comes to that, you can always drop it at Annani's feet. She will back you up."

His lips lifted in a sardonic smile. "That might help to keep my head attached to my neck, but that's about it. I would not be surprised to find myself the next occupant of that crappy cell."

"Yeah, you are probably right," she said as they stepped out into the corridor. "I'm curious, though, how did you manage to remove the camera feed from the bedroom?"

"I couldn't, not without pulling more people into this mess. You never know who might snitch."

"Oh, I see." Well, that was it for the sex then— even if she managed to get in the mood somehow...

"But"—he leaned to whisper in her ear—"there are no cameras in the bathroom. And I played with the one in the bedroom, repositioning it to observe only the bed. If you hug the wall as you enter and duck straight into the bathroom, the camera will not see you. I checked." He lifted his head. "Smart, ha?"

"The bathroom..." Amanda arched her brows.

"It's large, and I had Onidu schlep down a huge stack of towels." He winked. "You're welcome."

Okay, she could work with that—if needed.

"Thank you." She stretched on her toes and kissed his cheek, then grabbed his crinkly hair and pulled him down to whisper in his ear. "I truly appreciate what you've done for me, but if you ever tell anyone about any of this, Kian will be the least of your worries." She let him go.

"Don't worry, princess, your secrets are safe with me. Just remember, you owe me, big time."

"That I do. Whatever and whenever, I'm at your service." Not that she had a clue as to what he might need from her, but whatever it was, she owed him.

As they reached the door of the guest suite, Amanda grew nervous. Watching Anandur punch the code into the lock pad, she wiped her sweaty palms on her light gray trousers, then panicked, remembering they were silk and quickly checked for wet fingertips. Thank heavens, there were none. Tugging on the long sleeves of her white blouse, she held her breath as Anandur opened the door and went in first, keeping her behind him.

"I've got an early Christmas present for you, frog." He took a step to the side.

Dalhu's eyes widened as she came into view, and she heard his heartbeat speed up. He scrambled to his feet.

Anandur was on him immediately. "Take it easy." He pushed on Dalhu's shoulder until he sat back. "No sudden movements, buddy."

"Okay," Dalhu rasped. Eating her up with hungry eyes, he looked like a starved man who was just denied a juicy morsel of food.

"Hi," she said, running her hand through her hair. Why was it so awkward?

Anandur snorted and rolled his eyes. "Suddenly you two act like a couple of shy kids on a playdate when yesterday... well, you know." He wisely changed what he'd been planning to say next when Amanda pinned him with a hard stare. "Whatever. You go sit with your frog while I'll be over here, watching a movie, listening to it on my earbuds, full volume..." He pulled out a pair from his jean pocket and plugged it into his phone.

Making a show of twisting one of the dining chairs around to face the bar, he sat down with his back to them, plugged his ears, and lifted his booted feet to the bar's counter.

Anandur was turning out to be a real sweetheart. Who knew?

"Hi," Dalhu breathed as she sat down on the couch next to him.

"Are you okay?" He took her hand and enfolded it in his.

"I am. Are you?"

"Now that you're here... yes."

"I'm so sorry."

"Yeah, me too."

As they both stared at their entwined hands, there was no need to elaborate what they were sorry for.

All that could've been...

The what if...

When he reached a finger to wipe a tear from her cheek, she realized the mist in her eyes had coalesced.

"You look beautiful. This suits you." He brushed his fingers over her arm and then her thigh as if appreciating the luxurious fabrics.

Amanda chuckled. "You're just using it as an excuse to put your hands on me."

His eyes glinted with a fresh spark. "Guilty as charged, princess."

"About that..."

"Yeah, I know. No one could accuse me of aiming low, ha?" He sighed.

"So you're not mad at me for not telling you?"

"No, why would I be? I can't blame you for not trusting me with this."

There was a stretch of uncomfortable silence as they sat close enough to touch yet so far apart—separated by the deep chasm of their pasts, their clans' millennia-long conflict, their disparate social standing, their heritage. The weight of their deeds.

Except, none of that mattered when all she wanted was to get closer, to have him pull her into his arms and feel the strong muscles of his chest against her breasts and his large hands on her back.

"Do you still want me?" she whispered, gazing into his dark eyes.

"More than anything," he said softly. Dalhu's eyes briefly darted to Anandur before he grabbed the back of her neck and pulled her to his mouth, his other arm shooting around her back to mold her to his chest.

He kissed her as if he'd go crazy if he didn't, as if he had already gone too long without, groaning as she opened for him and drew his tongue into her mouth.

"There are no cameras in the bathroom," she whispered against his lips, desperate for the feel of his big, warm hands on her naked skin.

"Should we risk it? Won't it anger the Goddess? Your mother?" Dalhu allowed a little space between them so he could look into her eyes. "It's bad enough that I caused a rift between you and your brother. I don't want you to alienate the rest of your family on my behalf."

Such a noble sentiment from such a ruthless man. She wished her mother could've heard him. Dalhu didn't sound like a male bent on possessing her at all costs with no regard for the consequences.

Well, not anymore.

Trouble was, she couldn't decide whether this change came about because Dalhu cared about her so much that he was willing to sacrifice his own needs and wishes for her happiness, or because he figured it would be easier for him to just give her up.

"My mother was actually the one to arrange this behind my brother's back." Amanda smiled despite the seeds of insidious doubt that were taking root in her mind. "She tried to have the bedroom free of surveillance, but the bathroom and a clear path to it was the best Anandur was able to arrange."

Dalhu's brows lifted in surprise, his eyes softening with some indescribable feeling. "If I felt like worshiping at your mother's tiny feet before, now I'm moved to kiss the soles of her shoes." He kissed Amanda instead, lingering on her lips, then he brushed his mouth against her cheeks and her ears and along her jawline. "I can't believe she would do this for me, or that Anandur would help. I don't deserve this," he whispered, his voice sounding tortured.

"Sorry to disappoint, but they didn't do it for you. They did it for me." Amanda suspected he would prefer this take on things.

"Nevertheless, I'm grateful."

"We are providing one hell of a show for the guys in security," she breathed as he nuzzled her neck, the soft scrape of his fangs sending shivers all the way down to the wet spot between her legs.

Dalhu lifted his head, his eyes smoldering as his gaze drifted to the hardened peaks clearly outlined by the soft silk of her white blouse. He looked as if he had already stripped her and was ogling her naked flesh. His fangs elongated, extending over his lower lip, and she moaned—the sight of them bringing back memories of incomparable pleasure, but at the same time making her feel oddly vulnerable.

CHAPTER 15: DALHU

*A*manda went first, sneaking past Anandur, who made like a statue and pretended not to notice a thing.

But as Dalhu followed, the Guardian grabbed his arm. "You've got fifteen minutes. If you're not out by then, I'm coming in," he issued his warning, his hard eyes promising retribution.

Dalhu nodded and pulled away. Fifteen minutes would have to do.

Ducking into the bathroom, he found Amanda leaning against a stretch of mirrored wall, her beautiful breasts heaving with her panting breaths.

Dalhu was on her in a flash, tugging the blouse out of her pants and palming the satin-covered mounds.

Not good enough.

With an impatient growl, he shoved her bra up to get to her naked skin.

They both sucked in a breath.

Beaded with tight, dark nipples, her breasts seemed to swell for him. He cupped them gently, and when he moved his thumb back and forth across one hard tip, Amanda groaned, arching her back and thrusting more of her flesh into his hands.

"More," she commanded as her fingers threaded through his hair to pull him down.

"With pleasure." His fingers rolling and tugging, he dipped his head and took her mouth in a hungry kiss.

When he pinched, a rugged groan rose up from her throat, the back of her head hitting the wall and her hands losing their hold on his head, dropping by her sides.

And as he pulled her blouse up and over her head, Amanda seemed boneless—her arms lifting like a string puppet's, then dropping back to her sides.

She watched him with hooded eyes as he unclasped her white satin bra, leaving her upper body gloriously bare. Soon, he'd remove every last scrap of fabric covering her, but first, he needed a moment to gaze at her perfection.

Under his hungry stare, her nipples puckered even more. "I need your mouth on me," she breathed.

With a groan, he looped his arm around her back, clutching her ass as he heaved her up and took one tight, little nipple into his mouth. He suckled, rolling his tongue around it, then suckled again.

As his fangs scraped the sensitive bud, Amanda cried out, her back arching sharply. He moved to her other nipple and gave it the same treatment. She gasped, lacing her fingers through his hair and tugging his head closer.

When he had his fill of feasting on her breasts, he trailed kisses up her throat, letting her slide down his body so he could take those lush lips of hers again.

She murmured something incoherent as he dropped to his knees in front of her and with one hard tug on the waistband of her pants bared her completely. Sliding down her narrow hips, her lacy thong came down along with the trousers, the luxurious fabrics pooling like liquid silk at her feet.

Very gently, he placed a soft, open-mouthed kiss over her mound. She shivered, her hips swiveling wantonly, and as he extended his tongue and licked, her knees gave out and she braced herself on his shoulders—as if without the support she would've crumpled onto the floor.

It gave him a wicked idea.

Freeing one of her legs of the tangle of clothes they were trapped in, he lifted her foot to his shoulder, exposing her wet core. Both hands clutching her smooth ass cheeks, his grip was firm as he tilted her pelvis up to his hungry mouth.

It was so damn hot, the way Amanda watched him go down on her, and he pleasured her with blissful abandon, savoring her taste and the velvety softness of her nether lips.

"Fates, yes, don't stop!" she groaned.

His woman loved what he was doing to her, and he loved doing it... loved her...

"I need—" she began.

Before she had a chance to finish the sentence, he slid a finger into her tight sheath, then withdrew and thrust back with two.

"Dear Fates...ahh, yes!" Amanda cried out, her head once again banging against the mirrored wall behind her.

He chuckled, replacing his tongue with his thumb and rubbing lightly over her swollen clitoris. "Shouldn't it be, dear Dalhu?"

Lifting her head, she looked down at him. Her eyes were hooded with lust, but there was also a hint of a wicked gleam sparkling in them when she purred, "Dalhu, darling"—and grabbed his head with both hands, pulling him to her core. She undulated her hips, urging him to use his mouth, to thrust harder...

His woman wasn't shy about asking for what she needed.

More like demanding.

He would've enjoyed tormenting her a bit longer, but time was running out, and he had no idea what was left of the fifteen minutes Anandur had allotted him. He needed to bring her to a climax, and if there was any time left, maybe she could return the favor.

Sliding his fingers in and out of her, he pushed back in with a third, filling her, stretching her as he yearned to do with his shaft.

She let go of his head to pinch her own nipple and shoved a fist into her mouth to muffle the breathy moans which were gaining in volume.

Amanda was splendid, coming undone for him; a wanton, lustful, beautiful goddess.

And she was all his. Even if only for these stolen fifteen minutes.

With his eyes trained on hers, Dalhu closed his lips around the little bundle of nerves that was the seat of her pleasure and sucked it in.

As she orgasmed for him, she must've shoved that fist all the way inside her mouth, choking the scream that tore out of her throat. Still, he heard his name in that muffled shriek. And as her sheath kept rippling around his invading digits, he continued thrusting and suckling, wringing every last ounce of pleasure out of her until she pulled his head away.

With her fingers entwined in his hair, she tugged until she had him standing again, then kissed him, hard, her tongue invading his mouth.

He groaned, the idea of Amanda tasting herself on his tongue a major turn-on. Not that he needed the extra pressure. His cock was so engorged it was on the verge of exploding.

Her arms tightening around him, she pushed then pulled, turning them around, and it was Dalhu's turn to have his back pressed against the mirrored wall.

CHAPTER 16: AMANDA

*A*manda was far from done with Dalhu, the orgasm just whetting her appetite for more. Grinding her pelvis against his hard shaft, she all but fucked his mouth with her tongue, remembering to be careful around his fangs only after getting nicked.

She had some passing thought that her aggression might turn off a dominant male like him, but she just couldn't help herself. Everything inside her screamed, *more!*

She couldn't get enough of him.

Dimly aware that this lust was odd even for her, she cast the thought aside, her brain too scrambled with pheromones to think coherently.

Still, as she sank down on her knees and rubbed her cheek against his jean-clad erection, she had to accept that this was completely out of character for her.

No male had ever inspired her to pleasure him this way.

Amanda—the slut—had never given a blow job, not even once.

Why would she?

The guys she'd been with were of the disposable variety, and not entirely out of necessity. She had used them to get her fix and had deemed their services paid in full when they'd climaxed. Which of course, they all had.

Some, unfortunately, sooner than others.

The men, boys, had needed no extra stimulation, and she certainly had never felt close enough to any of them to perform such an intimate act just to reciprocate.

Dalhu's hands trembled as he cupped her face, lifting it away from his crotch. "You don't have to do this," he whispered.

"I want to." She kept her eyes on him as she popped his jean button free and began pulling the zipper down. Slowly.

"There is no time," he choked out.

No time? What the hell was he talking about? It wasn't as if he needed to be somewhere other than here. And she definitely wasn't late for anything—

"Time's up, frog, I'm coming in." Anandur rapped loudly on the door.

Oh, no he wouldn't.

Dalhu's muscles tensed and he swooped down, grabbing her arms in an attempt to get her up. She batted his hands away.

"Go away, Anandur," she hissed, her temper flaring. "I'll scratch your freaking eyes out if you dare to open this door."

There was a moment of silence before he responded. "As long as you're okay—"

"I'm fine. Now, get lost," she bit out.

Another moment passed.

"You're sure?"

"Fuck off, Anandur."

"Okay, no need to be rude, sheesh…"

She heard his soft footfalls as he left, and then the sound of the bedroom's door closing.

Dalhu let out a long breath and slid down the wall until his butt hit the floor, then scooped her into his arms and lifted her onto his lap.

"Did he ruin the mood?" she pouted.

Dalhu lifted up a little, pressing his hard-as-rock erection into her butt. "You think?"

"I still want to taste you," she purred, then averted her eyes, suddenly feeling shy. What if she sucked at it?

Sucked at it… She chuckled.

"What's so funny?"

"I was just thinking that I've never done this before and that I might suck at it. Get it? Suck?" She snorted.

Amanda felt his shaft jerk under her, growing even fuller. Tilting her head toward him with a finger under her chin, he whispered, "How is it possible?"

"How is it possible that I might suck at it? Or how is it possible that I've never done it before?" she taunted.

"The second one—"

She wanted to look away, but he held her chin firmly, forcing her to look into his dark eyes. "Tell me."

"I've never wanted to before." She shrugged, again trying to look away from those twin pools of darkness.

The smoldering heat and intense possessiveness made him look hard, ruthless, and she was suddenly very aware of being naked in his arms while he was still dressed.

Dalhu was scary, but in a good way—if it made any sense. Certain that he would never hurt her, his intensity and his ruthlessness titillated her, and she felt her core clench.

He sucked in a breath. "I…" He looked lost for

words. "I'm humbled that you're choosing me for your first time," he whispered.

Amanda cupped his smooth cheek, lifting a little to press a kiss to his lips. "There is no one I would rather do it for."

He closed his eyes when she wiggled out of his arms and reached inside his still unzipped pants to free his erection, hissing as his shaft jerked into her palm.

When she began stroking him, he lifted a little and pulled his jeans and boxers past his hips to give her better access.

Yanking them down the rest of the way, she moved to straddle his muscular legs. He spread them a little, forcing her to move her knees farther apart, his hard rod jutting, pulsing, beckoning her to touch it, taste it.

Licking her lips, she seized his shaft. He groaned in bliss, lifting up into her stroking hand as she rubbed her thumb across the head, spreading his own moisture down the length of him.

Gaze locked on his, she bent at the hips, gauging his reaction as she followed the same path with her tongue. He sucked in a breath, his eyelids briefly dropping before snapping open again—as if he didn't want to miss any of it.

He tasted good—a little sweet and a little salty but mostly potent—like the man himself. She went for another taste, licking him down and up like a Popsicle before returning back to the crown and circling it all around with long licks.

Operating on pure instinct, she hoped she was doing it right.

It was somewhat embarrassing to admit, but aside from her own experience at being pleasured this way—which considering the differences in anatomy wasn't all that helpful—she was ignorant on the subject. Even in theory.

As a lustful immortal, she was constantly horny as it was. Reading or watching anything erotic would've been like dousing gasoline on an already raging fire. She could not allow herself to indulge.

Now, she wished she had.

Though judging by Dalhu's groans and hisses, she was doing something right—not that it served as a true testament to her skill. As one of the comedians she'd once heard on the radio had said, "Flick it with a newspaper and it will do it for a guy..." Not to mention that he'd been referring to humans, who were pale, watered down versions compared to an immortal virile male.

"Oh, fuck, it feels so good." Dalhu bucked up as she licked the slit, arched his back sharply when she wrapped her lips around the head, and growled like a wild beast when she sucked it in. And as she moaned around him and sucked him even deeper, he banged his fisted hands on the floor.

Dalhu was magnificent in the throes of passion—carnal, animalistic—his big body shuddering, his leg muscles bunching, his T-shirt dampening from sweat.

And his fangs, sharp and long, had fully descended.

She was soaking wet just from seeing him like that and tried to ease the ache by rocking her hips in synch with her suckling.

He was getting closer, and as his shaft thickened inside her mouth, his hand shot to her head to hold her in place. Bucking his hips harder and thrusting deeper, Dalhu's growls were beginning to sound less and less human.

And yet, even though he seemed too far gone to think of anything other than his own pleasure, he didn't neglect hers. Bending a knee, he raised his leg up to rub at her wet sex.

She rocked her hips, grinding against his muscled thigh, the coarse hair covering it providing a delectable friction where it was most needed.

One hand gripping the base of his shaft and the other gently holding her head, Dalhu began thrusting deeper and faster. But she was so turned on, that instead of gagging, her throat muscles went lax under the onslaught, and she moaned and groaned around him.

With a muffled cry, he ejaculated—the hot jets of his seed sliding down her throat and stifling her own cries of completion.

He wasn't done, though.

With a sharp tug on her hair, he pulled her head up, and she gasped... not so much from the pain in her scalp as at the sight of his wild, glowing eyes and dripping fangs.

There was only one thing left for her to do.

She tilted her head and submitted her neck.

In a split second, his fangs sank in, the twin pinpricks burning like hell for the whole of two seconds before the venom hit and euphoria took over.

She climaxed again.

It took a few seconds or maybe minutes—she wasn't sure—before Amanda became aware of Dalhu's strong arms holding her flush against him and his hot tongue lapping at her throat.

She smiled and shifted, making herself more comfortable on his lap, then sighed. She was blissed out, wiped out... and just overall out.

Immortal sex was out of this world.

Dalhu had bitten her before, and he had brought her to a climax before as well. But not at the same time. And as it turned out, the two were definitely not one plus one.

More like two to the tenth power.

Dalhu nuzzled the spot he had licked so thoroughly before. "I'm sorry I lost it there at the end," he whispered against her neck.

"It was incredible." She breathed in, smiling and stretching. "Don't let it get to your head, but it was the best sex I ever had—by a huge margin. And we didn't even get to the main act yet. Imagine what that would be like."

Dalhu's wet cock jerked to attention under her butt. "Fuck, yeah...," he hissed. "Still, I hate that I lost control. I behaved like a crazed animal. Fuck, I was a beast."

"A very sexy beast," she purred, "and all mine. Mine to command and to serve my every whim." She looped an arm around his neck, pulling his head down for a kiss. "Right?"

"As you wish." He smiled down at her.

"Oh, you say the sweetest things."

CHAPTER 17: SEBASTIAN

*A*t his first-class private suite on Emirates Airlines, Sebastian Shar powered up his laptop. The lovely flight attendant had just cleared the dishes from the truly superb five-star dinner he'd finished, and before calling it a day, he wanted to check on the lineup of, hopefully, suitable properties for his new base in California.

The first on the list was a defunct all-boy boarding school. It had lovely if neglected grounds, with a school building and dormitories that were serviceable. But it was too close to the town it was named after.

The second was so perfect that it was almost too good to be true.

A Buddhist monastery near Ojai was closing its

gates after the number of monks had dwindled down to too few to manage the property.

At least this was the official story.

Sebastian suspected that running out of money had been the real reason behind it. He couldn't imagine that there was much demand for Buddhist retreats, and it didn't look like the monks had been producing anything for sale. Whatever, their mismanagement was his gain. The location was perfect, and the property was offered at a ridiculously low price.

The grounds, situated at the end of a long unpaved road, sprawled over gently sloping hills and were surrounded by a tall stone wall—topped with serpentine barbwire.

Apparently, a monk had gotten mauled by a mountain lion a few years back—the cat leaping with ease over the eight foot high stone wall. Following the attack, the monastery had added the barbwire, raising the height of the fence to well over twelve feet, and was now reassuring potential buyers that the wall was tall enough to keep mountain lions out.

Not really.

A big cat could jump over up to twenty feet. But this was not something that caused Sebastian concern. Predators were smart enough to stay away from more dangerous ones. There was no chance a cat would go after one of his warriors. A monk, on the other hand, must've been a tasty, defenseless treat.

The twelve-foot-high fence was good enough, and the place even came with a basement.

The monastery's few shortcomings were easy to fix. A new electric gate was needed, and on that note, it wouldn't hurt to electrify the barbwire as well. That way the place would be tightly secured—no uninvited guests getting in, and no prisoners getting out.

The main renovation, though, would be transforming the basement into a well-functioning dungeon. Used by the monks for storing produce and other staples, the basement was one big space, with random supporting walls and pillars strewn about.

Sebastian planned to turn it into living quarters for the girls he was going to provide his men with, applying the formula that worked so well for Passion Island to his own new stronghold.

There was no shortage of young, pretty junkies and runaways on the streets of LA. After all, other than the former Soviet Union, Los Angeles and New York were the main hubs for procuring fresh new flesh for the island—the typical customers showing a preference for the fair-skinned, blond, Slavic and American beauties.

For a short time, Sebastian would just divert the flow of supply to his new base.

Other than providing for the needs of his men, he envisioned turning a nice profit on the side. And as an added bonus, offering free and discreet sex services to his potential new business associates might be just the right sort of bribe—or in some cases extortion—to incentivize cooperation. In addition to the traditional monetary incentives, that is.

A few e-mails and phone calls later the deal was closed, and arrangements were made for the renovation work to start.

Now it was time for the fun part. Pulling out a crisp piece of white stationery paper, Sebastian began drawing a design for the dungeon.

He knew exactly how he wanted it. He was going to model it after an exclusive BDSM club in Amsterdam—one of his favorites. The club was housed in the basement of an old castle and was luxuriously appointed. Sebastian was not interested in replicating most of the common areas, but the layout and decor of the many private rooms was perfect for what he had in mind.

*I*t was late afternoon when Kian finally woke up.

Unbelievable.

He couldn't remember when was the last time he'd slept for so many hours straight. And as it turned out, his mother had been right—it was exactly what he'd needed. Without the exhaustion, last night's events and even her bizarre request to see the Doomer, although still troubling, no longer triggered an uncontrollable rage.

Instead, he wondered what she had learned.

But first thing first—he had some unfinished business with Syssi.

On that note, he was out of bed, showered, and dressed in a matter of minutes.

Well, the dressed part was an overstatement; he

pulled on some pants to go look for her, but was planning on shucking them as soon as he found her.

Smirking, he freed the top button and headed for the kitchen. Maybe he would start on the fun right there.

Except, instead of his lovely Syssi, he found Andrew sitting at the kitchen counter, drinking coffee and reading the morning paper.

Kian's morning newspaper.

Great. So much for his plans to use the counter for something other than eating... Or better yet, feasting on something other than food.

"Morning," Andrew muttered from behind the newspaper.

"Don't you mean afternoon?" Kian pulled out a barstool and helped himself to some of the coffee from the stainless steel, thermal carafe.

"Nah, it's still morning for me as well. I woke up not so long ago."

"Where is Syssi?"

"She left a note." Andrew pushed over a folded piece of paper.

To my two best guys, it said on the top flap.

Hope you slept well. Coffee is in the Thermos on the counter, and Okidu's delicious walnut pancakes are in the warming drawer. I'll be over at Amanda's. Come join us when you're ready.

XOXO

Damn, how disappointing.

With a sigh, Kian got up and headed for the warming drawer.

"Want some?" he asked Andrew as he piled a plate for himself.

"Sure."

Kian dropped the two plates stacked with pancakes on the counter and got some jelly and a can of ready-made whipped cream from the fridge.

As he sat down, Andrew passed him the headline news section, while he moved on to sports. Together, they ate and read in companionable silence.

Strange, how at ease they were with each other after butting heads like two bucks only yesterday. But as pleasant as this camaraderie was, Kian would have preferred to have Syssi sitting next to him while he ate his breakfast, or better yet, on his lap.

He missed her.

Wolfing down his pancakes at a record speed, he poured himself another cup of coffee to wash it down with. "I'm going to get dressed and head over to Amanda's. You coming?"

"Yeah, just give me a moment to put on my boots."

A few minutes later they met by the front door and crossed the few feet between Kian and Amanda's apartments.

Halting in front of her front door, Kian turned to

Andrew. "Before we go in, I just want to warn you. You are about to meet our Clan Mother, the only surviving goddess—"

"You're kidding me, a goddess?"

"That's right, I forgot you don't have the whole story, yet. So here is the very short version: the gods of old got wiped out by a nuclear bomb with only one goddess surviving. The mother of our clan. The bad guys, our enemies, are the descendants of another god, one who hated her. His son is their leader, and he carries on his father's mission to destroy her and the rest of us. The full version can wait for later."

"You keep saying that, but no one tells me anything. Truc?" Andrew arched a brow. "But whatever. What did you want to warn me about?"

"First and foremost, the fact that she is here is known only to a select few. She came when Amanda went missing, and to be with Syssi...Anyway, we can't risk our enemies finding out that she is here. So you talk to no one about it. Second, watch your language. Just behave as you would in the presence of a queen, and you'll be fine."

"What do I call her? Your highness? Your holiness?"

"No." Kian chuckled. "You can start with Clan Mother, and once she approves of you, she'll let you call her by her name, Annani."

"Got it."

"Ready?"

"Lead the way."

Kian rapped his knuckles on the door and pushed it open without waiting for an invitation to come in. If no one was giving him the courtesy, why should he?

"Oh, good, you're up." Crossing into the living room from the terrace through the open sliding doors, Syssi walked up to them and gave each a kiss on the cheek.

Yeah, a damn kiss on the cheek—that's all I get for all my troubles. But no worries, he was going to collect later...

"How is Amanda doing?" Andrew asked, craning his neck to see if she was outside.

"Um, she is taking a nap." For some reason, Syssi's cheeks reddened.

Something was afoot. "A nap? In the middle of the afternoon?" Kian lifted a brow, pinning Syssi with a suspicious stare.

"She had a rough night. A nightmare woke her shortly after she got in bed, and she couldn't shake it off for a long while. But eventually, the fatigue sent her crashing."

Syssi was hiding something, but Kian knew she wouldn't dare an outright lie in front of Andrew—the human lie detector.

"Perfectly understandable after what she has been through," Andrew murmured.

"Yeah, it is. Please, join us outside."

Out on the terrace, his mother welcomed them with a radiant smile, rising to give Kian a hug. "Thank you for bringing Amanda safely home. And you too, Andrew." She hugged the speechless Andrew.

The guy was stunned even though Annani's natural luminescence wasn't as visible in daylight, and her ancient, knowing eyes were hidden behind a pair of dark sunglasses. Still, there was no mistaking her palpable power and perfect features as anything but otherworldly.

"Andrew, this is my mother, Annani." Kian nudged Andrew with his elbow.

It took the guy a moment to respond as he glanced between Kian and the misleadingly youthful goddess. He dipped his head. "I'm honored, Clan Mother."

"Please, call me Annani, Andrew. You are part of the family now, and there is no need for formality." She patted his cheek. "Come, boys, take a seat. We have a lot to discuss." She sat back down and poured each of them a cup of black coffee.

"Your mother?" Andrew whispered, locking stares with Kian.

"Yes."

"And Amanda's…"

"Yes."

"Damn… "

Annani cleared her throat.

"My apologies, Clan Mother." Andrew bowed his head, belatedly reminded of Kian's instructions.

"Yes, well, you are forgiven." She sighed. "It is most unfortunate, though, that foul language became so prevalent in this age. It used to be that only the lowborn uttered such profanities. Now it is everyone. Even my dear children—who should know better." She lifted her brows at Kian.

He chuckled. "You see, Andrew? A mother is a mother, even a queen or a goddess. No matter how old her children are, she always finds something in need of improvement."

Annani smiled indulgently. But then she lifted her palm to end the casual banter, her expression reverting to its regal composure.

"There is an urgent matter that I need to discuss with both of you," she began. "I spent over an hour this morning chatting with Dalhu, and I was greatly troubled by the things he told me. But first, we need to address the issue of Amanda's safety."

Kian stiffened. "She is perfectly safe here in the keep."

"Yes, she is. But she needs to go back to work. Unfortunately, her identity is known to the few men remaining from Dalhu's original unit. He suggests we eliminate them before the reinforcements he asked for are scheduled to arrive, which he estimates will be over the next few days. He does not know the exact date."

"What makes him think his superiors are still in the dark about Amanda?" Andrew asked.

"He was in charge of this unit, and he did not disclose the information. The way their organization works, his men will do nothing without him ordering it. They will wait for him to return, or his replacement to arrive."

"And you believe anything that leaves a Doomer's mouth?" Kian humphed, crossing his arms over his chest.

Andrew cleared his throat. "It's actually not uncommon in cultlike organizations—correct me if I'm wrong to assume that this is the case here." He glanced at Kian, then continued when Kian didn't refute his assessment. "The brainwashing of the rank-and-file into blind obedience effectively nullifies a simple soldier's decision-making ability."

"And besides," Annani said. "Dalhu would not lie about anything that has to do with Amanda's safety. He is completely enamored with her, and he is committed to doing whatever it takes to safeguard her." She injected power into her tone, suggesting that as long as she didn't doubt the

Doomer's sincerity the subject wasn't open for debate.

Keeping his yap shut with difficulty, Kian met Annani's hard stare head-on.

She just smiled, shaking her head at him as if to mock his agitation. Then shifting her gaze to Andrew, she continued. "I believe that for the first time since this conflict began, we have a reliable source of information. Dalhu is more than willing to share with us all that he knows, shedding light not only on his former leader's machinations, but on what is going on in their backyard." Annani glanced briefly at Kian, anticipating a retort.

But as much as he hated to admit it, he was intrigued.

Annani sighed. "Except, for this information to remain relevant, it is imperative that his superiors never find out we have him, and that he is cooperating with us. With his whole unit gone missing—if we follow Dalhu's suggestion and take his men out—his superiors are going to suspect that someone was providing us with inside information."

"Yes, but what else can we do?" Syssi said in a small voice. "If you don't do as he says, Amanda will become a prisoner in here. She would hate it." She darted a nervous look at Kian, unsure she had a voice in this discussion.

Silly girl, of course she did. For better or worse,

she was now a member of the crew. Reaching for her hand under the table, he clasped it and gave it a reassuring squeeze.

Annani smirked as if she was waiting for just this objection. "I gave it a lot of thought and came up with a plan."

Oh, hell. Kian knew he was not going to like it.

"Instead of taking them out, which will entail entombing them in our crypt, I will fuddle their memories so they will remember nothing of taking Amanda's picture from Mark's home or staking out Syssi and Michael, not even the raid on the lab."

Annani raised her hand to shush Kian's objections. "To fill the gap, I will double their memories of the search for immortal males in nightclubs. Which, by the way, is the reason reinforcements are coming."

Her eyes turning fierce, she looked at Kian. "They need more manpower to cover an area as large as Los Angeles and its adjoining cities. And on that note, we need to issue a warning for everyone to stay away from clubs that admit indiscriminately. With some added security, the higher class members-only clubs should still be fine."

His mother must've lost her mind completely. "If you think I'll let you anywhere near those animals, you have another thing coming. This is the most harebrained idea you've ever come up with, and that's saying a lot." He pushed to his feet and began pacing.

"There is no other way, Kian. Sit down, please."

Annani waited for him to obey her command. "I am the only one that can affect other immortals' minds, and I will not be going alone. Andrew will accompany me, and you together with the other Guardians will be nearby. Far enough so the Doomers will not sense your presence, but close enough if anything goes wrong. Not that I anticipate any trouble; their simple minds will be like putty in my hands. I am only suggesting the escort for your peace of mind."

"So you plan on just walking up to their front door and knocking?" Kian threw his arms in the air. "What then? What if one of them isn't there? What if this is an ambush?"

"I can ask the Doomer some questions," Andrew suggested. "If there is any subterfuge, he won't be able to hide it from me."

"And I am going to use a disguise," Annani chirped, excited by what she no doubt thought of as a fun game. "Do not assume that I have not thought this through. I have a great plan. Andrew will pretend to be a health inspector, checking the house for mold contamination, and I will be the nurse checking each of the occupants for signs of mold poisoning—erasing their memories while I am at it."

"What makes you think they will not slam the door in our faces?" Andrew asked.

"Easy, you will tell them the inspection was prearranged with Dalhu. If they refuse, they will have to vacate the house and be put in quarantine. A very aggressive mold is suspected, and if indeed detected, it must be neutralized before spreading to neighboring houses."

"Very clever. We can show them some fake documentation to validate our official status. Even an inspection order. With one phone call, I can have the real thing delivered here in less than an hour."

"Don't encourage her." Kian shot Andrew a murderous glare before shifting to Annani. "I am not going to allow it. We do not go to the extreme measures we do to keep you safe and to guard your whereabouts, only to have you march head first into danger, treating a potentially disastrous situation like some silly little game."

In the silence that followed, Andrew and Syssi held their breaths as Kian held his mother's angry gaze. Eventually, Annani smiled, but it was the insidious, ill-boding kind of smile he was, unfortunately, all too familiar with.

"It is going to be done, my son. Your options are to either offer me your help or not. Whatever you decide, it has no bearing on my decision. As I have stated before, I do not require your permission, nor your assistance."

Grinding his teeth as he struggled to contain his outrage and stifle the bellow in his throat, Kian felt his facial muscles tighten. Knowing nothing he could say would change her mind, and hating that he was helpless to prevent this new disaster in the making, he turned to Syssi and Andrew with the faint hope that they might have a better chance of talking some sense into her stubborn head.

But by their expressions, it was obvious he was on his own. He wasn't sure, though, whether they were siding with Annani because they agreed with her, or because they feared the Goddess's wrath.

"What health inspection?" The Doomer who'd opened the door was talking to Andrew, but his eyes were trained on Annani's seductive smile.

Andrew flipped closed his inspector badge, which the Doomer had summarily ignored, and stuffed it into his jacket's inner pocket. Apparently, it had been a waste of time and resources to bother with obtaining authentic documentation. All that had been needed was a pretty girl with a smile. Not that Annani was a girl, but she sure as hell looked like one. And she had a killer smile.

Well, it wasn't a complete waste. With the badge and inspection order made and delivered on such short notice, Andrew had gotten to show off his impressive resources and connections.

Puffing out his chest, Andrew cleared his throat. "It was all arranged with Mr. Dalhu. Could you please tell him that Mr. Wyatt from the health department and the nurse are here to check for the mold infestation? I've already explained everything once. I would rather not have to repeat myself." Andrew affected a haughty, impatient tone.

Without acknowledging Andrew, the Doomer smiled at Annani and stepped back. "Mr. Dalhu is indisposed at the moment, but if you cleared this with him, then by all means, come in." He extended his arm and with a dip of his head invited Annani to go ahead. Following her inside, he left Andrew to trail behind.

"How can I be of assistance? Miss…?"

"Rebecca…" Annani pointed to the name tag pinned to the lapel of her short nurse's dress. "Nurse Rebecca McBrie."

Annani's outfit looked dangerously close to a naughty nurse's costume, even though it was the real thing and had been purchased from a de facto nursing supply store.

Cinched with a matching belt, the white dress accentuated Annani's tiny waist, and with its top buttons unfastened, the tops of her braless breasts were enough to cause a riot. White pantyhose and flat, white shoes completed the fetching outfit. She had tied her voluminous red hair in a loose bun, leaving a few wayward strands to frame her stunning face.

The Doomer was practically drooling, enthralled even before the Goddess used any of her formidable powers.

Apparently, she didn't need to.

Gazing up at the tall guy, Annani said, "Any room with a chair will do. And a door. I need to take skin and blood samples from each occupant." She smiled and winked. "In privacy." She touched the guy's chest.

The Doomer sucked in a breath. "Of course. Let me show you to the study." He reached for her arm.

"Hold on..." Andrew stayed the guy's hand. "First, I need to collect a few samples from the walls, and Nurse Rebecca is not allowed to draw blood unsupervised. Standard protocol." He'd promised Kian not to let her out of his sight. Not that he would've even without that promise. "Please, assemble the home's occupants first, and once everyone is here, we'll go ahead and test each one individually."

The Doomer narrowed his eyes and scrutinized Andrew for a long moment as if just realizing that there was someone besides *Nurse Rebecca* in the room.

Andrew managed to look down his nose at the guy with all the self-importance of a pompous city official, but as the seconds ticked off, he tensed, expecting the Doomer to smarten up and turn them away.

"What is your name, big guy?" Annani touched the guy's bicep. "Oh, my, you must work out, like a lot. Look at those arms." She brought her other palm up and tried to connect the fingers of her tiny hands around the muscle he was now flexing for her. "I cannot encircle it even with both my hands... the fingers do not meet... so strong...," she gasped.

"Edward." The Doomer grinned like an idiot, Annani's somewhat odd speech pattern escaping his notice as he flexed both arms for *Nurse Rebecca* to squeeze and *ooh* and *ah* over.

Hell, with how he was ogling her, a gorilla could've been crapping in the middle of the room and he wouldn't have noticed.

"So, are there any other big, handsome boys like you in the house? Or are you the only one?" Annani batted her eyelashes.

Damn, she is overdoing it. And calling the Doomer 'boy'? A dead giveaway.

"You'll be the judge of that." The Doomer pulled out his phone and texted. "They'll be coming down shortly." He smirked as if sure that he was going to win the good looks contest.

Unbelievable, the guy was buying her act.

Annani stretched on her toes and pulled him down to whisper in his ear, "I am sure none is more handsome than you, Edward... I love this name... Edward... so masculine," she breathed.

Were all men so gullible? Or was this particular Doomer exceptionally stupid? Annani's acting was bad, like in a third-rate porn bad. Yet considering her vast experience, she must've known what she was doing.

But come on, Andrew would've never fallen for that.

Perhaps she had been utilizing that influence thing. Though if she had, Andrew hadn't detected a thing.

Well, instead of observing Annani's antics, he should get busy with the samples he was supposed to collect.

Andrew snapped on a pair of latex gloves and proceeded to scrape some paint and dust from the baseboards at the entry and the living room, depositing the samples inside little plastic bags and scribbling notes on the tags attached to them. All along, he kept Annani in his line of sight.

When all six Doomers surrounded tiny Annani, he got nervous. But he had nothing to worry about— the other five were just as dumb as the first.

Or maybe she was just that good.

"I'm done with the samples, gentlemen. Let's proceed with Nurse Rebecca's tests," he announced as he pushed through the wall of meat to get to Annani.

"I'm going first," Edward volunteered. "Wait here for your turn," he instructed the others.

As he took Annani's elbow and led her to the study, Andrew followed, closing the double doors behind him.

"Grab a chair, darling," Annani said, depositing her medical kit on the long table in the center of the room.

The study was more of a library, with shelves full of leather-bound books, a few oversized leather recliners, and two chairs at each side of the long mahogany table in its center.

The Doomer calling himself Edward sat next to where Annani arranged her tools and laid his forearm on the table.

She flicked on the closest reading lamp and trained the light on the crook of his arm, then leaned and touched his shoulder. "Are you nervous, big boy?"

Now Andrew could detect a faint hypnotic undercurrent in her melodic voice.

"Not at all, sweetheart." It took the Doomer a second or two to lift his stare up from her cleavage and gaze into her eyes.

He was hers the moment their eyes met.

The Doomer seemed paralyzed, not even blinking.

Annani said nothing as she looked into the guy's eyes, absentmindedly brushing her fingers through his hair as if to soothe him while she played with his memories.

Fascinated, Andrew watched the Doomer's face. There was something familiar about the guy, and he had a nagging feeling that he had seen him somewhere before.

Andrew would've dismissed it as a strange déjà vu, but as each of the Doomers took his turn submitting to Annani's ministrations, the feeling grew stronger.

It took all six for his brain to make the connection. Without their beards, they were not as readily recognizable, but eventually it all snapped into place.

As it turned out, the twelve recent visitors from Maldives he'd been searching for were Dalhu and his men.

Serendipitous or what? Finding the answer to the mystery was an unexpected bonus to this little stint.

And who said good deeds went unrewarded…

Once the Goddess was done, she closed her medic case and waved the six stupefied guys goodbye.

"Piece of pie." Annani high-fived Andrew the moment he closed the front door behind her, then pumped her small fist and whooped like a cheer-leader whose team had won.

She was bursting with energy as they entered his car and all through the drive back to the keep, excited over what she perceived as a wonderful adventure. "A refreshing break from my routine," she confided in him. "Oh, Andrew, I cannot remember when was the last time I had this much fun. I have been stifled in this role I have been stuck in: playing the queen mother, hiding away in a remote place with barely any mortals to play with."

She sighed. "It is not who I am on the inside. I crave adventure, excitement."

If she weren't who she was, he would have patted her knee for reassurance. But come on, she was a freaking goddess, for God's sake, and for all he knew, she might've smote him for daring to touch her.

But as she continued without pause, he realized she only wanted his ear and wasn't expecting a response.

In this, Annani was a typical woman.

Finally, she stopped long enough for him to ask the question that was bothering him. "I'm curious. What exactly will these Doomers remember and what will they forget?"

Annani shrugged. "They will remember nothing about Amanda. I erased, or rather muddled, their memory of ever seeing her picture or even taking it from Mark's home. I also muddled their memories of going after Michael and Syssi, and of searching Amanda's lab. Other than these, I didn't mess with anything else."

"Did you leave them the memory of our visit? And why? Isn't it dangerous? They will know what you look like."

"Think about it. When I was done with one of them and proceeded to the next, we were still there for the first one to remember." She said it as if he was a little dimwitted for not figuring it out. "If it were possible to thrall them all at once, then maybe I might have been able to do it. But one at a time? No. And besides, they are males. So they will only remember that Nurse Rebecca had a lovely bosom. Not much more than that. No thralling required." She smirked.

Andrew chuckled, she had a point.

"Today was great. I feel alive." Annani threw her hands in the air and began singing a merry tune in a foreign language he couldn't place.

Not that he cared. Her siren voice was so beautiful, he could've listened to her endlessly. Andrew idly wondered if that voice of hers could be used as a weapon. Probably. It had an enthralling quality, powerful enough to lure men to follow wherever she wanted to lead them.

A smile tugged at Andrew's mouth. Was that the real story behind the siren's song legend? The voice of a goddess? Or goddesses?

As he parked in the underground garage, Annani didn't wait for him to open the door for her. She was out of the car before he even cut the engine. No doubt running to tell Amanda the good news.

Andrew waited for Kian and the other Guardians to file out of their SUV before heading up.

The Goddess's ebullient mood evidently hadn't waned in the short time it had taken Andrew and Kian to get up to Amanda's penthouse. Prancing around in her short nurse's dress, and tiny, white nurse's flat-soled shoes, she was in the middle of recounting the story for Amanda's eager ears.

Andrew found that he was fond of the Clan Mother. With how she looked now, exuberant, like a young girl in a Halloween costume, it was easy to forget that Annani was the most powerful being on earth.

Earlier, as they'd readied to embark on this evening's information containment mission, Andrew had braced himself for having a lousy time in her company, expecting the Goddess to have a condescending diva attitude. But it turned out that she was a riot to be around. And besides her little tiff with profanity, the Goddess seemed to embrace contemporary culture wholeheartedly and was surpassingly well versed in many of its nuances.

Though somewhat intimidating, Annani was a lively and pleasant companion. In fact, if she were an agent, he wouldn't have minded having her as a partner. He had always known the power a beautiful woman had over men, but he'd underestimated to what extent. Someone like her would have made his work so much easier, keeping men stupefied and easy to manipulate.

Andrew sighed. If he were ten years younger, he would've petitioned his superiors for a drop-dead-gorgeous female partner. But his time as a field operative was a thing of the past, and he had no need for a partner. Gorgeous or not.

Sitting on Amanda's deep-cushioned couch, Kian glared at his mother. Probably still sulking over her flagrant disregard for her own safety. Or maybe it was her brushing off his protests and overriding his authority that had him fuming. Most likely both. Andrew sympathized. If it were his mother or his sister, he would've felt the same.

The guy was holding Syssi glued to his side as if he feared she might get infected by Annani's recklessness.

It didn't seem to bother the Goddess, though. "You should have seen Andrew, flashing his fake inspector badge with such pompous superiority, just as a city official would. Your brother is a fantastic performer, Syssi," Annani chirped as she paced around, too excited to sit down.

Andrew lifted off the chair to offer a mock bow. "Thank you, thank you all." He affected a snobbish British accent to everyone's delight.

Except Kian's.

It seemed that a scowl would be the guy's only expression for the foreseeable future.

Pushing up from her chair, Amanda wiped a stray tear from her eye. "You have no idea how much I appreciate what you have done for me. I love you all. Thank you." She sniffled, first reaching for her mother and pulling her in for a hug, then Syssi and the reluctant Kian—saving the biggest hug for Andrew. "I'm sorry that I missed your command performance." She flashed him her beautiful smile.

Damn woman, why did she have to get this close?

As her soft breasts pressed against his chest, and her belly brushed against his arousal, the contact sizzled through his skin as if it was branding him.

And that smile…

Oh, God, that smile…

The heat sliding through his veins crept all the way up his neck and was about to engulf his ears. Great, just what he needed. Blushing like a schoolboy for everyone to see because a girl that had a crush on someone else had smiled at him.

Been there, done that, wrote the book, sold the rights to the movie.

That first time, he'd been only ten years old. Not that being a kid had made it any less traumatic. Karina, he was never going to forget her name, the girl he had a crush on since kindergarten, had seemed to like him too, giving him false hope. But by the end of fifth grade, she'd told everyone she liked Ben Brook and had obliterated Andrew's young heart.

Lesson learned: until Amanda made up her mind one way or the other, he was not going to succumb to her considerable charms.

No siree, Bob.

Easier said than done, though. No man in his right mind could help wanting a woman like her. Andrew detested the useless pining. As the saying went, want in one hand, shit in the other... Andrew had a bad feeling about which one he was going to get.

Desperate to divert attention away from himself, he gently dislodged Amanda's arms and turned to face Annani. He cleared his throat. "I don't want to spoil your good mood, but I am curious to hear what else the Doomer had to say, specifically about their organization."

"Well, yes," she said, plopping down onto one of the overstuffed armchairs. "First, I need something to drink. I feel a little parched. Would you be a dear, Kian? And pour me something sweet and tangy? You know what I like."

"Sure." Kian managed not to sound surly. He pushed off the sofa. "Anyone else?" he asked as he headed to the bar.

"I'll pass," Andrew said.

Amanda lifted her hand. "A margarita for me."

"Syssi? Anything for you?"

"I'll have the same."

After mixing the three margaritas, Kian handed one to Annani, then delivered the other two to Syssi and Amanda.

Annani waited patiently for Kian to pour himself some scotch and go back to his seat next to Syssi.

Sweeping a quick gaze over her audience, she made sure everyone's eyes were trained on her before she began. "Navuh has his own little island somewhere in the Indian Ocean, and no one aside from him and his sons knows exactly where it is. The mortal pilots transporting people and goods to and from the island are heavily thralled to guard the secret, and the planes they fly are windowless. Everyone and everything is carefully checked for tracking devices before being allowed on board, then checked again upon arrival."

"Clever…," Andrew muttered.

"Indeed." Annani nodded gravely and continued.

"The island serves as the home base for his army of immortals, which just as we had suspected has close to ten thousand brutally trained warriors."

"Damn," Kian bit out.

Ignoring his slip, Annani sighed and took a long sip of her drink. "The island is also known as Passion Island; a large-scale, lucrative brothel, secretly serving a select clientele of very rich, powerful mortals. The women, serving these clients and the soldiers are snatched off the streets from all over the world and forced into servitude. They can choose, however, between sexual service or manual labor as cooks, maids, servers and the like. Once enslaved, they are never allowed to leave the island. A highly guarded portion of this brothel is a prison within the larger prison, segregating the Dormants from the rest of the compound. Paired with mortal clients who possess traits valuable to Navuh, mainly physical size and brutality, they are bred to produce boys to be turned and serve in Navuh's army, and girls who remain Dormant and serve in the brothel once they turn fifteen, continuing their mothers' task of producing the next generation."

Amanda sucked in a breath. "That's terrible. No wonder Dalhu was appalled by the idea of a female Guardian."

"Well, Doomers' opinion of women is not exactly a newsflash," Kian snorted. "Inferior, and good for serving males and breeding only." He pinned her with a condescending look.

"No, that is not why he was so aghast. Though before I gave him a chance to explain, I too accused him of misogyny."

"Then what?" Syssi lifted a brow.

"He asked who was the moron that came up with the brilliant idea of employing females in the Guardian force, considering the kind of enemy we're facing." Amanda shot Kian an accusing look.

He shifted uncomfortably.

"He said that even before he met me and switched loyalties, if it were up to him, he would have never, ever allowed an immortal female to fall into the clutches of his brethren. He even went as far as saying that he would have killed whoever needed killing to free her. And this is a direct quote." With a small satisfied smirk, Amanda held Kian's gaze until he looked away.

Andrew chuckled. *Score one for Amanda.*

But wait, the Doomer looking good was the opposite of what was good for Andrew... Nevertheless, the guy had just gained esteem in Andrew's eyes.

Kian wasn't ready to concede, though. "And you believed him? That's the other thing we all know about Doomers—they are obdurate liars—they say whatever they think you want to hear because they have absolutely no regard for you, no respect. For them it is like lying to a dog or a cow—it doesn't count!"

The guy had a point. Some of Andrew's missions had taken him into that part of the world, and he had personal experience with this kind of culture. Being a good liar and successfully pulling one over on your enemy was something to be proud of, a badge of honor. And the inferior fool who believed the lie deserved what he got. Be it being cheated out of something, or death.

Well, score one for Kian.

But the match wasn't over yet, and Amanda wasn't ready to fold. Getting up and marching to stand in front of her brother, she pointed a finger at Kian. "Yes, I did. You might think me a fool, but I am far from it. And you, who did not exchange even one word with Dalhu, still think you know him better than I do. He is not like the others."

"That is enough, children," Annani cut in. "Amanda is correct. Before you pass judgment, Kian, you might want to go and talk with Dalhu because we just cannot afford to dismiss everything he says as a lie. The information he disclosed is too valuable. And although I have no idea what we could do for these poor women, we are still their only hope. Maybe, if we all put our heads together, we could come up with a rescue plan."

Kian crossed his arms over his chest, glaring at his mother and sister in stubborn silence.

"I could go with you," Andrew offered reluctantly. "Provide my human lie detector services."

The last thing he wanted was to help Dalhu, his number one rival for Amanda's affection. But Andrew had a feeling the guy had been forthright, and if so, the information he was providing was invaluable. And the only way Kian would act on it was if he was assured of its veracity.

Hence, Andrew felt morally obligated.

Damn.

Amanda turned to him. "Lie detector? What do you mean?"

Syssi snorted. "Yeah, he is really good at that. You have no idea how hard it was to grow up with him. On the rare occasion that I tried to hide something, he always knew. I just assumed that I was a terrible liar."

"You are." Andrew chuckled. "But even the best cannot deceive me face to face. I don't know how, but I'm never wrong. Except, over the phone. I'm not so good without visual clues."

Rubbing her chin with her thumb and forefinger, Amanda made an *hmm* sound. "Interesting, most immortals have some special ability—some even more than one. This was actually my hypothesis for identifying potential Dormants, and you've just reinforced it. Syssi has strong precognition ability, Michael is a good telepath, and you, Andrew, are the lie detector."

Annani clapped her hands. "Problem solved, then. With Andrew's special talent to aid you, you will have your proof of Dalhu's loyalty." She looked pointedly at Kian.

That frown he had going on rode the guy's brow even harder, turning his face into a cruel mask. "As you all gang up on me, caviling my hostility toward that Doomer, you forget something. That male, the one you are all rooting for with such enthusiasm, is Mark's murderer. It might not have been his fangs that delivered the deadly dose of venom, but they might've just as well. He was in charge—the one who ordered it."

Kian looked each of them in the eyes before pinning Amanda with a hard glare. "Face it, sister mine; that Doomer you seem so taken with, the one you allowed access to your body, murdered your beloved nephew."

In the silence that followed, Amanda's eyes widened with consternation and her tall body began to tremble. She slapped a palm over her mouth as if she was about to retch.

On a surge, Annani got up and reached for her daughter, pulling her into her arms. Too short to reach over Amanda's shoulder, she leaned sideways to glare at Kian with eyes that could freeze lava. "Explain the realities of war to my son, Andrew," she bit out.

It was an exceedingly awkward situation. On one hand, Andrew's rival had been dealt a potentially fatal blow. Score one for Andrew. On the other hand, Kian was being a total jerk, and Amanda looked devastated.

The facts of war, as Annani had so succinctly put it, were that shit like this happened. Warring factions made peace, and former enemies became allies—often to join forces against a common adversary. But be that as it may, in this case, it was too close and personal.

"No one needs to explain the facts of war to me," Kian grated as he heaved himself off the sofa. "Come, Syssi, let's go home." He offered her his hand.

With an apologetic glance at Amanda, Syssi let him walk her out.

"I am sorry you got caught up in this drama, Andrew." Annani sighed. "I just want you to know that I am grateful for all your help. It was fun." She smiled a little before leading Amanda out of the room.

Letting himself out, Andrew walked up to the single elevator door and punched the button to call it up. The few things he had left over at Kian's could be picked up some other time. This evening, it was time to go home and do some serious thinking.

Or soul searching as it were.

Question was, would he do the right thing and try to talk some sense into Kian? Or would he do the selfish thing and let Kian cool down on his own?

And while Kian was taking his time to come to terms with the situation, Andrew's rival would be temporarily out of the race, giving Andrew the opportunity to make his move for Amanda.

It might be his only chance.

CHAPTER 20: AMANDA

The storm of conflicting emotions that kept Amanda tossing and turning all through the night eventually had given her one hell of a headache.

Or maybe it was all that crying before she'd finally fallen asleep. After Kian had forced her to face the fact that her paramour was responsible for her nephew's murder, she'd cried for hours.

To be frank, the thought had flitted through her mind before, but she'd shoved it aside, doing the cowardly thing and refusing to let it sink in. And until Kian had shoved it in her face, she'd gotten away with it.

Same way she usually got away with ignoring almost everything she considered potentially disturbing.

After her son's tragic death... was it almost two centuries ago? It still hurt so bad... it had been the only way she'd managed to keep herself afloat and not sink into depression. Except, with time, she became so adroit at this strategy that anything disconcerting or unpleasant no longer registered at all.

It was like she was wearing a coat of Teflon—nothing stuck.

And nothing got absorbed either.

Which, come to think, might have been the reason behind the hollowness she felt inside.

Nothing about her was real. She was a made-up persona. Most of the time she thought nothing of it; on the contrary, she thought of herself as larger than life. But the truth was that she was kind of cartoonish.

Pretty on the outside, empty on the inside.

The problem was, she had no idea who she really was.

After pretending for so long, she had forgotten. And what's worse, Amanda feared she wouldn't like the *real her* if she ever found her.

The persona she had created was great, and she liked being that woman. Carefree, dramatic, lustful, smart, not to mention beautiful... pretty cool, if she may say so herself. Unfortunately, the pretense didn't run deep enough—more than skin deep, but not all the way down to her shriveled soul.

With a sigh, she gave up on sleep and got up.

Dawn was on the horizon, the wispy rosy-pink like a whisper of hope against the backdrop of gloomy darkness. Donning a warm robe, Amanda opened the sliding door to the terrace and stepped out into the chilly air. As the cold seeped through the fleece, giving her goose bumps, she tightened the robe against her body.

A faint ocean scent was riding on the breeze, cutting through the morning fog and evoking a strange longing for the sea—a voyage that would take her far away from this place and the hard choices that were weighing her down.

Choices.

Not really, more like lack of.

Now that Mark's murder was firmly pinned on Dalhu, Amanda couldn't stomach the idea of being anywhere near the guy.

The thing was, she couldn't imagine going back to her old life either. Or living without what Dalhu had given her...

The intimacy, the sense of connection, the mind-blowing pleasure...

The unrelenting devotion.

What were the chances of her ever finding something like this again? A man who made her feel like a princess for real? Forever...

Andrew?

Yeah, there was some attraction there. But she was well familiar with this kind of superficial connection. Amanda had nearly two centuries of experience with it.

It didn't reach all the way down to the essence of her.

Heck, it wasn't even skin deep.

And though Andrew might believe differently at the moment, it wasn't the real thing for him either.

Trouble was, until he found it, Andrew would not know that this wasn't it, and would keep trying to win her.

If only she had never crossed paths with Dalhu, she wouldn't have known better and could've been happy with Andrew.

Everything would have been so much simpler then...

Until... one of them happened to find the real thing, and then their lives would've turned into a nightmare...

Yeah.

Syssi had been absolutely right when she'd said that relationships were complicated, people were complicated, and not everything could be resolved with great sex.

Amanda leaned over the railing and breathed in, searching for the faint ocean scent that was quickly dispersing along with the morning fog.

She needed to get away.

But five o'clock in the morning was too early to make calls.

To pass the time she took a long bath and then spent a couple of mindless hours shopping for shoes on the Internet.

At eight, she phoned Alex.

Still too early for a guy that worked nights, but whatever, he owed her.

As the phone kept ringing and ringing, she almost hung up, but then Alex finally answered. "What's going on?" he rasped.

"Morning. Sorry to wake you up, but I need a favor."

"Amanda? Thank the merciful Fates you're okay. Everyone was looking for you. I didn't know you'd been found. What happened?"

Damn, she didn't know how much he knew. "Yeah, they found me. Though I wish they didn't." It wasn't a lie, wasn't the truth either, but good enough. "That's why I'm calling. Can I borrow your yacht for a few days? I need some time alone, and with my intrusive family that's not going to happen unless they can't reach me. Like in the middle of the ocean."

His answer came after a short pause. "Sure,

though I'd appreciate you telling them where you're going this time."

"I will. Promise. So is it okay with you? Or do you have plans for it yourself?"

"No, not for the next couple of weeks. How long do you need it for?"

"Only a few days, less than a week for sure. On Monday, I'm going back to work. So I'll be back Sunday evening at the latest. Does it work for you?"

"Yeah…" He hesitated.

"Don't worry, you know I'll cover all the expenses." Alex was such a miser. On the other hand, fuel for a boat this size was expensive, and she shouldn't expect him to pay for it. Loaning her the boat with its crew was enough.

"Good, but that's not the problem."

"Then what?"

"You know my crew is all female, right?"

"No, I didn't know that, you naughty boy."

"And although I have no problem with you there, I would appreciate it if you didn't bring any guys with you. My girls are not for sharing."

"No worries. It's actually perfect for what I have in mind. I'm taking a break from men."

Alex snorted. "Why? What happened?"

"Long story, but yeah… no guys."

"When should I tell my captain to expect you?

And where would you be heading? She needs to stock up on supplies."

"I don't really care where, just out to sea. Maybe down the coast toward Baja. Would a couple of hours be enough time for her to prepare?"

"I'll call Geneva right away—not the city, my captain—and if she needs more time, I'll call you."

"Wonderful, thank you. The name of your yacht is Anna, right?"

"The one and only, my pride and joy."

With that settled, Amanda scribbled a quick note for Annani and left it on the kitchen counter.

Hopefully, her mother would understand why she needed to get away and forgive Amanda for not spending more time with her during her rare visit.

Amanda promised to make it up to Annani as soon as she regained some sanity.

Half an hour later, she was out the door with a large satchel over her shoulder and a carry-on rolling behind her.

Thank heavens the penthouse's elevator could be made to go straight down to the lobby without stopping at any of the other floors. The last thing she needed was for one of her relatives to come along for the ride and start asking questions.

Waving the security guys goodbye, she hurried into the taxi waiting for her in front of the building.

"Good morning, Miss. Marina del Rey? Right?"

The cabbie verified the destination she had given his dispatch as he loaded her luggage into the trunk.

"Yes, thank you." She waited until he opened the door for her.

Once the taxi pulled out, Amanda relaxed into the seat.

Mission accomplished, she was free.

Fates, it felt good.

To be free to do whatever she wanted. With no one to censor her, no one to criticize her or her choices, and no one to answer to.

No angry brother. No enemy lover.

Free as a bird.

What a shame Captain Geneva couldn't head out to sea right away.

Well, the important thing was that she managed to flee the coop without getting caught, and she didn't mind spending the hour or so eating breakfast in the café overlooking the water while the captain and her crew prepared the *Anna* for the trip down to Baja. Or maybe to Catalina, she could decide later. As long as the boat was out of the marina, with her onboard, the destination didn't really matter.

CHAPTER 21: SYSSI

"*D*on't go." Syssi caught Kian's arm as he tried to sneak out of bed.

"I'm just going down to the gym." He bent to kiss her cheek, expecting her to let go. Instead, she grabbed on and pulled him back.

Wow, cool. She hadn't expected him to budge.

Hey, this was new. She was growing stronger. There was no way she could've done this before her transition. Still, she was pretty sure that if her new and improved physique hadn't taken Kian by surprise, it wouldn't have been so easy. Next time, he would be ready for her increased strength.

"You're not going anywhere. I hate waking up in an empty bed." She pouted and snuggled up to him, her hands going to his warm, bare chest.

Last night, Kian had made good on his word and

then some, and the only reason she wasn't sore all over this morning was the venom's magical healing properties.

Or maybe it was her new, better, and stronger body.

Hey, she might be faster too. She should join Kian in the gym and test her speed on a treadmill.

"I thought I exhausted you last night."

"What gave you that idea?" Her hand trailed lower.

"The T-shirt and panties said it all."

"Yeah? What did they say?"

"Get away from me, you brute. I need to sleep, you insatiable sex machine...," he said in a high-pitched voice.

Syssi laughed. "True. True. And how surprisingly perceptive of you."

He rolled on top of her, bracing his weight on his forearms. "When you returned from the bathroom wearing these things, crawled into bed and started snoring right away, it would've been impossible even for an insensitive jerk like me not to get a clue."

"I don't snore." Syssi felt her cheeks warm. *Bummer*, she thought Kian's sexcapades had cured her of her embarrassing tendency to blush, but apparently not.

"Yes, you do. And your little kitten snores are as cute as the rest of you."

"A cute kitten? That's what you think of me?" She took hold of his erection and began stroking. *How about that for cute...*

Kian smirked before dipping his head and taking her mouth in a hungry kiss. That was all it took for her nipples to pebble and her cotton panties to get moist.

"How about my little sex kitten?" He nuzzled her neck.

She pushed up her hips to rub her hot and achy core against his shaft. "That's better...," she breathed as he scraped his fangs up and down her neck.

Damn, Kian knew all of her triggers by now, every erogenous point. He could probably get her from zero to orgasm in under a minute.

"My kitten is hungry for more?" Kian's hand trailed under her T-shirt to palm her breast.

Suddenly, she didn't want any barriers between them. "Take it off." She wiggled under him in an effort to free the shirt from under her butt.

"Hungry and impatient. I like it." He gave her nipple a little tweak before helping her out of the shirt.

Once he bared her, Kian took a moment to ogle her nakedness. "I can never have enough of this. If I had my way, you would wear nothing when we are alone... all day long."

"Absolutely nothing? Not even stilettos?" she taunted.

His erection twitched. "Uh, that's one hell of an image, you naughty girl. I'll allow the high heels, and a diamond wedding ring and choker to go with them…"

The vivid picture he painted in her head had her flood her panties. "Is that a pervy proposal?"

"I'm not asking, I'm stating a fact. You're mine." He cupped her through the soaking wet cotton.

"And I have nothing to say about it?"

"You already did." He sneaked a finger under the edge, stroking her swollen, wet flesh before pushing the thick digit inside her.

Syssi moaned, arching, her hips going up for more.

"I'll take it as a yes…," Kian's voice deepened with his arousal. He didn't wait for her answer. Instead, he dipped his head and took a nipple between his lips, suckling and finger fucking her into a frenzy.

"Yes, oh yesss…," Syssi hissed as his teeth gently closed around her nipple.

She was going to come like that, but it was okay. Before this was over, her wonderful man would make her come again. And again…

CHAPTER 22: ANDREW

On his way to the office, Andrew stopped by the Beverly Hills mansion.

"Hello, Edward." He flashed his inspector badge again. "Remember me? I'm Inspector Wyatt with the health department. I was here yesterday to collect mold samples."

"What do you want?"

"I need to collect a few more samples."

"Why?"

Without Annani to scramble the guy's brain, he wasn't as eager to cooperate. Well, maybe the Doomer would respond better to a different approach.

Dropping the condescending mannerism, Andrew ran his fingers through his hair. "Who the hell knows. The guys in the lab don't give a shit if I need to drive an hour out of my way to collect some more dirt for them to play with. You know how it is. I'm just following orders."

The Doomer still didn't give any indication that he was going to let Andrew in. Evidently, friendly wasn't going to cut it, but a threat might.

"Look, Edward, the test results came inconclusive. I either bring them more samples to test, or they are going to put in a request for the guys in hazmat suits to quarantine the house."

That did the trick. "Okay, but be quick about it."

Problem was, with the Doomer breathing down his neck throughout the *inspection*, Andrew barely managed to plant one tiny listening device in the living room.

Better one than none, though.

With the anticipated reinforcements arriving soon, someone would no doubt make contact with Dalhu's remaining crew. And when it happened, Andrew might learn something.

It was a shame he had not thought of the idea until this morning. It would've been easier yesterday when all of the Doomers had been busy drooling over Annani.

But no harm done.

From now on, Andrew's little spy would keep

transmitting, and anything that was said in its vicinity would be recorded.

Hopefully, he could learn of the Doomers' new location.

Andrew felt a twinge of guilt over the unauthorized use of government resources for his private sting. But it wasn't as if he could tell his bosses what was going on and get them on board with the fight against this new and bizarre threat.

He'd be sent to a psych evaluation and suspended from his job before his boss finished rolling his eyes.

But the clan needed his help.

Andrew didn't have the whole story yet, but it was obvious his new relatives were outnumbered and outmuscled by their enemies. They could really use his particular expertise.

Perhaps he should quit the agency and go work for them.

Kian would love to have him, and the pay would most definitely be better.

Some of the operatives he had known had chosen to move into the private sector. Instead of accepting a glorified desk job once they were deemed too old for the field, they were still out there and making shitloads of money.

But if he quit, he would lose access to the most valuable of resources—information.

True, he had friends that would do him a favor here and there, but it would be just crumbs. Compared to the vast pool of data he had access to with his high-security clearance, it would be a drop in the bucket.

No, quitting the agency wasn't an option. But Kian would have to fund some equipment. Using his access to government data to help the clan was one thing, using its gadgets was another.

A tracker here and there or one simple listening device he could get away with, but more missing equipment would trigger a red flag at accounting, and he'd have internal affairs on his ass.

Still, keeping his job and at the same time helping the clan would be a tough gig to pull. He'd be working endless hours. And if he were to run missions for the clan, he'd have to miss work days at the agency.

As he had done for Amanda's rescue.

The long hours didn't bother him. It wasn't as if he had anything better to do with his life. Always better to keep busy than go home to an empty house and stare at the stupid tube until it was time to sleep.

The problem would be taking time off.

True, Andrew hadn't used his vacation days in God knows how many years, and he had accumulated quite a lot. Nevertheless, he would run out of them pretty quick if he went on missions for the clan.

He would have to make it work, somehow, because for the first time in God knows how long, Andrew was excited about something, anything, and it felt good.

CHAPTER 23: SYSSI

"Come in," Annani chimed.

Syssi would never get used to the quality of that voice.

Heavenly. As befitting a goddess.

"Good morning," she said as she opened the door to Amanda's apartment.

"And a lovely morning to you too. Did you have breakfast already, my dear?"

Judging by the dark sunglasses perched on her pert nose, Annani was about to take her breakfast out on the terrace.

It seemed the Goddess couldn't get enough of Southern California's sunshine. Not a big surprise considering her home was in Alaska. Still, with her sensitivity to the bright light, it must've been a mixed bag of goods.

"Yes, I did, but I would gladly have another cup of coffee." Syssi followed Annani out, joining her at the table that was being set by... not Onidu, but someone who must've been his brother.

More like a twin.

"How many brothers are there?" Syssi reached for the coffee press while sneaking a surreptitious glance at the guy, but she only got his profile.

"Brothers?" Annani tilted her head, her dark red brows arching above the black frame of her sunglasses.

"Onidu and Okidu and now... I'm sorry, I don't know your name..." As he turned, Syssi looked up at Annani's butler, searching his face for dissimilarities between him and his two other brothers.

"Oridu, madame, at your service." He bowed at the waist. "Would there be anything else Mistress might require?" he addressed Annani.

"No, thank you." Annani sounded like she was choking down giggles.

"What's so funny?" Syssi asked as soon as Oridu disappeared inside.

"I see that Kian did not tell you. He must have forgotten in all the excitement," Annani chortled.

"Didn't tell me what?"

"The Odus, they are not brothers, well, at least not in a strict interpretation of the term, though they were probably made by the same person."

Wasn't that the definition of brothers? Or half-brothers at the least?

Annani must've realized Syssi's confusion. "What I mean by made, is manufactured, constructed, not born of a mother and father."

"Like clones?" Syssi scooted to the edge of her seat. This was so exciting, though somewhat morally disturbing. But to see a living proof that cloning humans was possible? Mind-boggling.

"No." Annani paused to think. "I guess their creator might have used some genetic material to build their outer shell. And if I would hazard another guess, it was probably his own."

She chuckled. "Funny, I often tried to imagine the genius behind the Odus, and yet, it never crossed my mind that he might have created them in his own image."

What Annani was trying to say was starting to sink in.

Except, no way...

"You mean that they are some kind of robot? It's impossible... or more accurately, impossible with current technology." But God only knew how... *now, that's funny...* how advanced the gods' technology had been.

"You are right. We do not have the technology either. The Odus are marvelous, practically indestructible, invaluable. They were a wedding present from my Khiann, and they were considered an ancient relic even then."

Khiann must have been the young husband Annani had lost so long ago. Her voice had faltered when she'd said his name. For her to mourn his death thousands of years later, their love must've been indeed legendary.

"And speaking of weddings"—Annani perked up —"it is time we started to plan yours."

"Oh, no, Kian and I haven't discussed anything yet. It is way too early to be even talking about a wedding, let alone planning it."

"You mean to tell me that there is any doubt in either of your minds? Or that the subject did not come up?"

"No… and yes…" The damn blush was taking over her face again.

"I do not understand. Is it a no, or a yes?"

Oh boy, how to answer when she wasn't sure herself. "No, I don't have any doubts, and I'm pretty sure Kian doesn't either. And yes, the subject came up… sort of…"

"What do you mean, sort of? Has Kian proposed or not?" The Goddess leaned forward, her displeasure evident even behind the dark sunglasses.

Why? Oh, why? Did she have to probe like this? Like I'm going to tell her about Kian's pervy proposal.

Oh, hell, here goes nothing.

"He did, but I think it was meant as a joke." Syssi's ears were so hot they were in danger of catching fire.

Annani smiled and leaned back. "Then it is settled."

"But what if he was only joking?"

"Trust me, child, men do not joke about things like that."

Most men wouldn't. But Kian's kinky mind had been busy imagining her in nothing but stilettos and a collar, and attempting to make it sound less pervy, he had exchanged it for a diamond choker, throwing in the wedding ring as a bonus.

"I see you are still unsure." Annani pursed her lips and produced a smartphone from a hidden pocket in her dress. Before Syssi had time to process her intentions, the Goddess's small fingers flew over the screen and she pressed send.

"What have you done?" She would be so humiliated if Kian laughed at the idea. And why wouldn't he? It was absurd to talk about marriage so soon.

"Do not worry, my dear. I only asked Kian when and where he wants to hold the wedding."

As Syssi's mouth did an imitation of a fish out of water, Annani's phone pinged with a return message.

"That was quick." Annani smiled as she lifted the phone from the table. "Let me read it to you: As soon as you can make the arrangements and get all the clan members here. First wedding. We celebrate big."

"Can I see that?" Syssi wouldn't have put it past Annani to invent this.

The Goddess handed her the phone.

Yep, there it was, black on-screen. "I don't know what to say." Syssi cradled the device. "Could you send me a screenshot? I want to save this."

"As soon as you give me my phone back." Annani chuckled.

Reluctantly, Syssi did. "Is Amanda still sleeping? I need to talk to her…" Syssi felt like she was falling down the rabbit hole again. She needed Amanda to keep her from going into full panic mode.

Why was all this talk about a wedding making her so anxious? It wasn't about second thoughts. Syssi had none. Kian was the only man she would ever want. It was just that everything was moving too fast.

What was the rush?

She wasn't pregnant, so why the shotgun wedding?

"No, Amanda is not here. My daughter decided to take some time off by herself." Annani sighed. "Poor girl."

"Where? When?"

And how could she? The deserter. Apparently when the going gets tough, Amanda splits, probably to go shopping.

"She did not say. But Amanda has her phone with her so you can call her with the good news. I am sure she will love to help us plan the joyous event."

Planning any grand party, and Syssi's wedding in particular, was definitely something Amanda would love to sink her claws into, and she was much better suited for that than Syssi. Problem was, Syssi didn't feel ready for a wedding, even if someone else took over the preparations.

"Why the rush, though? I don't understand. Is it about propriety? I would have thought that your..." She corrected herself. "...our people don't concern themselves with things like that."

Annani sighed and leaned to take hold of Syssi's hand—the one holding a spoon and endlessly stirring creamer into her coffee. "My dear Syssi, I understand that you are overwhelmed and that everything is moving too fast. And considering that you and Kian have all the time in the world, literally, you do not understand why I am rushing you."

"Exactly."

"In part because it is my nature. Once I make up my mind about something, I do not procrastinate, I do not examine and question my decision, I move forward. I trust my intuition because it is smarter than me."

Annani's eyes shone with ancient wisdom as she patted Syssi's hand. "Action is a forward movement, fear and procrastination are not. You have already made the decision to tie your life with my son's. Do not let fear hold you from moving forward."

"It's not about fear..."—*yeah, it's totally about fear*—"I just prefer to progress at a slower pace."

Annani wasn't fooled. "Do not fret, child, trust your instincts."

Syssi sighed, she was going nowhere with the Goddess, and it seemed that resistance was futile when dealing with Annani. "So what is the other reason for the rush? You said it was only in part about moving forward."

"Excitement, hope. Do you realize that yours and Kian's will be the first clan wedding? The best cause for celebration we've had in ages? This is why Kian wants to invite everybody, and why the party we are going to plan must be grand—unforgettable."

Syssi felt herself relax a little. That kind of a party would take months to plan, maybe even a year, which would give her time to get used to the idea. And in the meantime, Kian would get to know her better, and hopefully still want to stay with her. The worst scenario she could imagine was if Kian regretted his decision. Which he still might, once they spent more time together.

"How long do you think planning and producing an unforgettable party will take?" *Please say a year...*

"To plan a ball for close to six hundred people,

including travel arrangements for those who will come from out of town, we will need at least two weeks."

"Two weeks?" Syssi croaked.

"Maybe I could shave off a day or two, but no less than ten days."

Oh, boy, it was getting hard to breathe through the surge of panic. "My parents... are in Africa..." she managed a whisper, or rather a whimper... "My mother is a doctor, she cannot just get up and go on such short notice, and travel is complicated."

"It is not a problem. We will send another doctor to cover for her in her absence and charter a private jet to bring your parents here. Same for their return trip."

Evidently, enough money could move things forward very quickly, and Annani was going to move mountains to have her grand celebration in two weeks or less. If Syssi wanted a say in her own wedding, she'd better stop chickening out.

If you can't fight them, join them. Right?

"What are we going to tell my parents?"

"About what, dear?"

"Who you are, who I am now, why the shotgun wedding?"

"We can pretend to be mortals, and you could tell them that you fell in love with a Scot, who comes from a large family, a clan, and that you are rushing the wedding because his mother has to return home, which is true. I cannot stay here indefinitely."

Syssi snorted. "Yeah, right. I can just imagine introducing you as Kian's mother. You look younger than him. And the rest of the clan? You think my parents wouldn't notice that everyone seems to be no older than thirty-five?"

"Yes, I see, you are right. Which means that you will have to tell them the truth, and then before they go home, someone will have to thrall them."

"Maybe I shouldn't invite my parents at all. Instead, I could send them a postcard from my fake honeymoon in Hawaii, informing them that I've eloped." Her parents would most likely prefer for her to do it this way. She would save them from being inconvenienced by their only daughter's wedding.

Bitter, much?

"It is up to you. Whatever you choose to do, Kian and I will support your decision. But if you decide not to invite them, just bear in mind that you are only getting married once, and later on you might regret not having them witness your wedding."

Yeah, Annani had a point. After all, it wasn't as if Syssi was estranged from her parents, or didn't love them. She shouldn't let her resentment over petty grievances cloud her judgment or influence such important decisions.

But on the other hand, the issue of them

attending the wedding wasn't the only thing to worry about regarding her parents. In the long run, the real problem would be how to explain why she wasn't aging.

Makeup?

Refrain from seeing them altogether?

"I need to think about it."

"You do that, dear. But do not take too long, because if you decide to invite them, we will need time for the travel arrangements."

"Yes, I know."

"How about we ring Amanda now? If we are to pull it off successfully, we need her on board." Annani handed Syssi the phone. "Go ahead, call her," she prompted.

Syssi narrowed her eyes at the Goddess. "I see what you're doing. You want to lure her back with the wedding plans."

"But of course, what is wrong with that?"

"Absolutely nothing."

CHAPTER 24: AMANDA

On board the *Anna*, Amanda lounged on the top deck with a martini in one hand and a tablet in the other—reading the same paragraph for the third time.

Her mind just refused to stay focused on the romance novel, even though it was the latest release by one of her favorite authors. And it wasn't as if reading about someone else's love tribulations was upsetting her. After all, misery liked company. However, unlike the novel's protagonist, Amanda's problems wouldn't get resolved at the end of the three hundred and some pages, and her story had no chance of culminating with a happily-ever-after.

But her troubles, as grave and as daunting as they were, weren't the reason for her inattention.

Since her first moment onboard, Amanda

couldn't shake the feeling that there was something fishy about Captain Geneva and her crew. And if these females were Alex's type, then there was something wrong with the guy as well.

The *Anna's* all female crew was an unpleasant bunch of butch lesbos if she ever saw one. The vibe they projected was absolutely nasty.

The gay part didn't bother her, and it wasn't as if anyone could accuse Amanda of having a prejudice against her own gender. To the contrary. Although she loved men for sex, she preferred the company of other women. And not only because she could carry on an intelligent conversation without lust scrambling her brain.

In her experience, and contrary to popular belief, women were by far more honest and trustworthy than men.

Unless they were vying for the attention of the same guy. Then all bets were off. But when chasing tail, men weren't any better, and the whole bros-before-hoes was another urban legend.

At first, Amanda had thought she was imagining the nasty looks. Then, as Captain Geneva had made the introductions, and Amanda had realized all six women were Russian, she had speculated that cultural differences might've been responsible for the cold welcome.

Then again, she had known quite a few Russians

in her day, and although a scowl was the Russians' most popular expression, the people she had met were also easy to joke and laugh with once they'd grown comfortable around her, especially after a few drinks. Not these girls, though. They'd remained unfriendly, if not outwardly hostile.

Apparently, onboard the *Anna*, the cold war was still on.

Except, she hadn't tried to get them drunk yet.

Hmm, alcohol might improve their disposition. If she wanted to enjoy her trip, she should throw a party and get the bitches drunk. Hopefully, the free booze would cure their hostility.

"Hey, Lana," she called the one who was supposed to be a stewardess. A tall, leggy blonde that kept an eye on her as if suspecting Amanda of planning to abscond with the silverware.

"What you want?"

Now, how is that for polite?

"Do you have a karaoke on board?"

"Why?" Lana of the many words asked.

"Maybe I want to throw a party, get you girls to loosen up a bit so you'll pull the sticks out of your butts."

"Ha, you lucky Alexander said to treat you nice."

"Or what?" *Bring it on, bitch...*

"Or you find out what happens to stupid American girls like you." Lana smiled menacingly.

"Lana!" Geneva barked. "*Zat'knis!*" Shut up.

"*Shto?*" What? Lana shrugged. "*Ona nie ponimayu.*" She doesn't understand.

Oh, she understands all right, suka—bitch.

"*Idi suyda,*" come here, Geneva commanded.

"*B'lyad…*" Fuck, Lana muttered and stomped up to Geneva.

The captain said nothing besides glaring and pointing a finger toward the stairs leading down. Once Lana disappeared down the stairwell, Geneva walked over to Amanda.

"I apologize for Lana's rudeness. She will be punished." Geneva dipped her head then pivoted on her heel.

"Wait…"

"What?"

"What are you going to do to her?"

"What disciplinary action I decide on is none of your concern, Dr. Dokani."

Oh, so now I am Dr. Dokani…how cordial.

"Look, Captain, Geneva, I don't know what's going on, but I don't understand why you are all so, how to put it nicely, bitchy. Did everyone go into her period at the same time or something? I heard it happens when several females live together."

"Again, I apologize. Is there anything I can do to make you feel more welcome?" Her eyes colder than a Siberian winter, Geneva looked like she was holding herself in check by a thread.

"Yeah, give everyone a bottle of vodka, I'll gladly pay for it. But seriously, what have I done to earn such animosity? I'm a pretty cool chick once you get to know me."

Geneva dipped her head and took in a long breath. "It's not really about you. Please don't tell Alexander I told you this, but we were promised two weeks off. And believe me, the crew needs it."

Alex had mentioned something about not needing the *Anna* for the next couple of weeks. But Amanda had a feeling the captain was deflecting with a convenient excuse.

For now, though, Amanda would give her the benefit of the doubt.

"I see, sorry I've ruined your vacation plans. Now I can understand why you guys are pissed off at me. How about I double your pay for the time I'm here? Will that improve everyone's mood?'

"You'll do that?"

"Sure, I want to enjoy myself and I am willing to pay for it. Give me the names and numbers, and I'll wire the money to each girl's account. And put the vodka on my tab as well." Suddenly, Amanda was struck by a brilliant idea. "One bottle for each girl and one for me. I bet a hundred that this American can outdrink all of you Russians."

Geneva's smile was the first Amanda had seen since getting on board. "In that case, American, you will have to pay for at least three bottles of vodka for each. One bottle is not a challenge for a Russian."

Yeah, like these girls could handle three bottles.

Amanda pretended being horrified for about five seconds, then narrowed her eyes at Geneva and smiled. "You are on, suka." She watched as Geneva's eyes widened.

"You speak Russian?"

"Nah, just a few curse words." No need to reveal her cards, yet, or ever. For some reason, Amanda suspected there was more going on than met the eye on board the *Anna*.

Things didn't add up.

Why hire a graceless, foreign crew for a luxury blue water yacht that must've cost Alex something in the range of twenty-five million?

Save some chump-change on wages?

Come to think of it, where did he get the kind of money needed to buy a boat like this?

His share in the clan profits was enough to keep him in style, but not this kind of style, and his club, although successful, wasn't making this kind of money either.

Was Alex really dealing drugs as Kian had insinuated?

Well, tonight, she was going to get the crew

drunk and ask some questions. With an immortal's high tolerance for alcohol, even the infamous Russians had no chance of besting her in a drinking competition.

*I*t was late evening when Sebastian's plane taxied up to the sleeve at Tom Bradley International Terminal in Los Angeles.

Immigration took forever, but everything went without a hitch. An hour and a half later, he and his assistants walked up the ramp where they were greeted by a uniformed limo driver with a sign that read "Mr. Sebastian Shar."

Slugging along the freeway in LA's infamous traffic, it took another hour to reach their accommodations for the night—the renowned Beverly Hills Hotel.

"Nice," Robert said as he looked around the elegant lobby.

"Wait until you see the suites I've reserved for us, each with a bedroom, a separate living room, and a balcony." Tom glanced at Sebastian. "You said to go for the best..."

"Yes, I did." He'd meant for himself, but what the hell, it wasn't like the cost was going out of his own pocket. Let the men enjoy. "Only the best for my team. Go settle down. I'll see you tomorrow morning." Sebastian pocketed the card-key to his suite.

"Eh, boss..." Tom stopped him. "What about some ass? I don't know about you, but I need some, and so does Robert. He is just too shy to say anything."

"Call the concierge, tell him you're with me and you need special accommodation. He'll know what to do."

"Sweet."

Sebastian had tried the service before. Unfortunately, it couldn't provide for his particular tastes. And it wasn't a good idea to indulge with an unreceptive hooker anywhere other than the island. Even with the fast healing the venom facilitated, it took time for the evidence to disappear, and the last thing he needed was to call attention to himself by getting arrested.

Besides, in a hotel, there was no way to contain the screams other than gagging his victim, which he preferred not to do. It was like watching a movie without the sound.

And what fun was that...

Which meant no room service for Sebastian. He had to scratch his itch elsewhere.

But as the saying went; where there was demand, for the right amount of money, there was supply.

The first time Sebastian had visited LA, he had found a club catering to his extreme tastes and had been a loyal member, or customer as it was, since.

"Tomorrow, nine, my suite. Until then, I bid you good night," he told his men and headed to his room.

Let them think what they would.

Sebastian waited until the bellboy brought his luggage, then grabbed a quick shower, changed into something appropriate for his planned activity, and called for a taxi to take him to the club.

CHAPTER 26: DALHU

The passage of time progressed at a different pace in rooms without windows, Dalhu reflected as he stared at the ceiling. Or maybe it was the isolation and lack of activity that made it seem as if he'd been stuck in there forever. Though in reality, it was less than forty-eight hours since he had been imprisoned.

And twenty-one hours thirty-two minutes since he'd last seen Amanda.

But who was counting?

Fuck.

Why had she abandoned him?

She could've at least called. There was a phone in his fancy prison. And although it wasn't connected to the outside world, only to some guy in security, she could've obtained the number with ease.

Or not.

Maybe her brother had forbidden it.

Probably.

It was the most likely explanation.

Amanda had loved their bathroom interlude, and Dalhu could think of no reason for her to stay away unless she had no choice.

He was going out of his mind with worry.

And boredom…

How many movies could a guy watch?

The only other entertainment option was a large assortment of video games, but he'd never learned how to play.

Not that he had any desire to.

Grown men shouldn't entertain themselves with boys' games.

By now, he'd hoped Amanda would come see him again. But the only visitor he'd had for the past day and a half was the stoic butler who had been bringing in his meals.

Strange that they were sending the small man by himself with no Guardian backup. Not that Dalhu had any intention of hurting the guy, still, they had no way of knowing it. And although the Goddess hadn't seemed to regard Dalhu as a murderous abomination, her son definitely had.

Not that the fucker was wrong necessarily.

But the butler didn't appear to have a problem

with Dalhu. Polite, as if serving an honored guest, the stout little man wasn't nervous around him at all.

Getting some information out of the guy, though, had been a no go. Same for the significantly less cordial guy in security.

No one would tell Dalhu anything.

Still, when the butler showed up again with the evening snack, Dalhu gave it another try.

"Hey, my man, does anyone plan on seeing me tonight?"

"I do not know, sir."

"And Amanda, is she well?"

"As I have said before, I do not know."

Well, it was worth a try.

But then the butler added, "I have not seen the mistress today to ask about her well-being."

"Why? Where did she go?"

"I do not know, sir."

Fuck, the guy didn't deny that Amanda was gone.

Had her brother had something to do with it? Had he sent her away to prevent any further contact between them?

Anger rising to the surface, Dalhu managed to appear calm until the little guy left. Once he was alone, though, the urge to destroy everything in his vicinity became almost overpowering. He didn't. All that trashing the room would have achieved, aside from releasing the excess steam, would have been to prove Kian's point, and Dalhu was not about to give the fucker the satisfaction.

Still, the barely contained rage needed an outlet.

A good, rigorous fight would've helped, or even a long run, but as those were not an option, Dalhu dropped to the floor and began a series of fast push-ups.

He slowed the pace after the first thousand, but kept going without rest until he was drenched in sweat.

It wasn't enough, though.

It took another three thousand sit-ups until he was finally ready to quit and hit the shower.

"*H*ave you talked with Amanda?" Kian asked, giving the comforter a tug from his side and stretching it nice and flat over the bed the way Syssi liked it.

For some unfathomable reason, Syssi had insisted on making the bed herself instead of leaving the task to Okidu.

It wasn't like the butler needed help with the house chores; after all, he never tired and never slept, which thanks to Annani, Syssi was now well aware of.

Kian still couldn't believe he hadn't explained about Okidu. But the truth was that he'd never regarded his butler as anything other than a person, often catching himself giving Okidu incomplete instructions because it was so damn easy to forget the guy's limits.

And besides, considering the whirlwind of events following Syssi's transition and Amanda's kidnapping, no wonder the subject had never come up.

It had slipped his mind.

Not that Syssi had made a big deal out of it. In fact, Syssi was not the type to make a big deal out of anything other than the really important stuff.

His sweet Syssi, he smiled at her from across the bed. He was so lucky to have her.

And he had to admit that doing this little morning chore together felt kind of nice. Intimate, in a familiar sort of way. Kian was looking forward to countless mornings just like this one.

Each time he'd woken up with Syssi's warm body in his arms, Kian had thanked the Fates for the gift of her—the happiness and gratitude setting a positive tone for the rest of his day.

And whether it was her chest or her back that was pressed to his front, he had no particular preference—both were equally enticing.

Now that Syssi wasn't allowing him out of bed before she was up, he was making love to her every morning as well as every night.

Good times. Good times indeed.

"No, I'm giving her space. I wanted to call her

yesterday, you know, after your mother sprung that whole wedding thing on me, but then I decided to wait. Amanda didn't get away just to have me heap my troubles on top of hers. She has enough stuff to sort out."

Troubles?

"I'll pretend I didn't just hear you say that."

"What?"

"Marrying me is trouble?"

"Oh, you know what I mean. But here..." Syssi climbed on top of the just-made bed and crab-walked on her knees to where he was standing on the other side. Grabbing him by his shirt, she pulled him to her mouth and kissed him until they were both starved for breath. "Better?" she panted.

"A little..." Kian lifted her in his arms then spread her out on the bed, covering her with his body like a blanket. "Now, this is better." He began trailing kisses, starting with her sweet lips, going down to her chin, then her neck, until he reached her breasts. Cupping her through her shirt, he pushed them together and licked the valley in between.

Syssi giggled. "Oh, shoot, now we'll have to make the bed again."

"We could wait, you know..." Kian gazed into her smiling eyes, so full of love, so adoring. "I want our wedding to be a source of joy for you, not anxiety."

"I know, right? My heart is fully on board with it, but I can't stop thinking about how little we know each other. And after a lifetime of cautiously examining each and every decision, no matter how trivial, I'm having trouble with just jumping headlong into the most important one. It's not like I'm having doubts. You know my heart belongs to you, forever. I'm just a big, fat, chicken, that's all."

"First of all, you're not big and not fat. And as to being a chicken, well, you are my scrumptious, hot chick." Kian gave the valley between her breasts another long lick. "Yummy." He smacked his lips.

"How come you're not freaking out? I thought men were supposed to be the commitment-phobes."

"I've waited for you for close to two thousand years, and now that I have you, I'm done with waiting. I love you, will always love you, and will never stop loving you. I know it like I know that the sun will rise in the morning and set in the evening, and that spring will lead to summer. No doubts. You were, are, and will be the only one for me."

Syssi's eyes misted with tears. "Wow, I have no words."

"You don't have to say anything. Your eyes and your body tell me all I need to know. For now. Later, when you find the words, you'll tell me." He quoted her own words back to her. The words she'd spoken to him that first night they had spent together.

Her eyes foggy with tears, she reached a hand to cup his cheek and smiled. "Well, my love, it seems you found the most beautiful words. And to think you claimed you're not a romantic."

"I had professed to be an uncouth brute, and a crude, insensitive jerk. I've never said anything about not being romantic. Though, I'm just telling it as it is."

"I love you so much," Syssi whispered.

"I know."

"No more doubts, I don't need any more time, let's do it—a grand wedding to eclipse them all."

"What have I done? I've created a monster!" Kian gasped in mock horror, then kissed the living daylights out of her. "But seriously," he said after letting her take a breath, "if you need more time, that's okay. Just not too long—I'm not a patient guy."

"No, I'm diving in, headlong. And if it means that Amanda's little vacation is cut short, tough. I'm calling her, and she'd better pack her bags and come home right away. I need her."

"That's my girl." Kian kissed Syssi's forehead. "Beautiful, lush, smart, and brave."

"Brave?"

"Yes, brave. Bravery is not about the absence of fear. It's about facing it and conquering it."

The little smirk on her face told him that she liked his compliment, but then she said, "If this is so, my love, you need to back your words with actions.

It's time you faced your own fears and conquered them."

This was not the answer he'd been expecting.

And what did she mean by that?

"Did you just call me a coward?" Kian pinned her arms to her sides.

"I wouldn't dream of it." A mischievous smile was tugging at her lips. "You might spank me if I did," she breathed.

Imp.

"I'm going to spank you anyway...because you fucking love it."

"When?"

"Not before you tell me what that facing my fears is all about."

Turning serious, Syssi sighed, and with a little shrug freed her arms. She then cupped his cheeks with her soft palms. "In your case it is not about fear. It's about facing the demons of your past and rising above them. You need to go talk to Dalhu."

And wasn't that a complete mood spoiler.

Damn Doomer.

"I know. And later today I will. But I want Andrew to be there. Without him to verify it, I won't believe anything that comes out of that scum's mouth."

"Text him, I'm sure Andrew would gladly offer his lie detector services."

CHAPTER 28: ANDREW

*A*ndrew closed the Maldives file with mixed feelings. He hated that there was nothing for him to report, or rather nothing he could report. The war between the two immortal factions was not a threat to national security, and therefore not something his agency was concerned with.

Under normal circumstances, he would've forwarded the file to the police or the FBI, but there sure as fuck was nothing ordinary about this.

But be that as it may, the new file assigned to him was so massive that he was glad to be rid of the old one. Someone higher up had either been tipped off, or just had the smarts to realize that airport security should include in its screening not only the travelers, but also the thousands upon thousands of employees; from cleaning crews,

mechanics, and other service personnel, to stewardesses and pilots.

Right now, he had close to two hundred
employee files to investigate, and that was only the
initial sweep of potential suspects from just one
airport.

If his boss had thought Andrew could do it all by
himself, the guy was delusional.

And as if Andrew hadn't had enough on his plate,
this morning Kian had texted him, asking Andrew to
stop by any time that worked for him. Today. Apparently, his unique talent was required for verifying
the Doomer's story.

There would be no overtime for Andrew this
evening, at least not on his official job.

At five sharp, he headed out, ignoring the raised
brow or two his coworkers sported. They would
have to get used to him no longer being the last one
to leave the office.

Gone were the days when he had stayed late
because there had been nothing and no one waiting
for him at home, and he would work, or hit the
downstairs gym, until it was late enough for him to
join his friends for some drinks at the bar.

Now, he had a whole bloody clan that needed
him. And surprisingly, the added responsibility felt
good. Or maybe it was the sense of belonging—of
being part of a tribe.

Even if only on its fringes, he thought as he eased into the designated guest parking of the luxury high-rise. Andrew wondered what it would take for him to get access to the private one underground.

Hell, he still didn't even know Kian's last name.

True, with a name like that it wasn't as if the security guard manning the reception desk at the lobby would ask Kian who?

As soon as Andrew said he was there to see Kian, the two guys at the front desk snapped to attention. One got busy on the phone while the other pointed Andrew to the waiting area. "Someone will be here shortly to escort you upstairs."

Ignoring the guard's suggestion, Andrew did a little walk about the lobby, taking in the opulence he'd been too agitated to notice the first time he'd been here. The space, some thirty feet tall and spanning most of the building's footprint, was all marble, glass and mirrors. Dotted with contemporary leather sofas and chairs that were grouped around glass tables, and big, green trees he wasn't sure were real or fake, it looked like the lobby of a high-end hotel.

But what interested him most were the extensive security measures.

There were the requisite cameras, though as well hidden as they were, it took someone who knew what to look for to find them.

The reception slash guard station, as well as any point of entry into the building proper, was separated from the lobby by thick, bulletproof glass. And the only door to the other side had none of the standard key-card entry pads or even a handle. The only way for the thing to open was for a security guy to buzz you in or out.

Clever.

But it didn't end there. Besides the three elevators visible through the glass partition, Andrew knew there were three more on the other side. Though to get to them from the lobby, one had to not only be buzzed in but have a key-card to another inconspicuous door—labeled *Maintenance.*

Waiting for his escort, Andrew didn't watch the bank of elevators this time, but the beautiful flower arrangement farther away at the back wall, or rather the alcove to its right.

The one leading to a short corridor and the door labeled *Maintenance.*

He didn't have to wait long until a burly guy emerged from that alcove, but not one of the Guardians Andrew had met before. Still, the man, or immortal, had no trouble figuring out who Andrew was. Though not necessarily because he knew who to look for, but simply because Andrew was the only one on the other side of the glass.

"Bhathian." The guy offered his hand.

Apparently, no one here bothered with last names. Which kind of made sense for those hundreds of years old. Last names were, after all, a recent invention, evolving from the medieval naming practice which had been based on an individual's occupation, or where they were from, or the name of their clan.

"Andrew." Shaking Bhathian's hand, Andrew omitted his own surname. When in Rome, do as the Romans do… and all that.

The big guy wasn't one for small talk, and they made their way to the private bank of elevators in silence.

After getting out on basement level three, Bhathian stopped in front of the first door that was made of glass as opposed to the solid metal of the other doors they'd passed by. "First, let me check if Kian is ready to see you."

Behind the double door was a large, nicely kitted-out office, with a conference table in its center, and a desk at the back, where Kian was busy on the phone.

He cast Andrew an apologetic glance.

"Let's go." Bhathian pulled out his phone and lifted it up for Kian to see, then waited until Kian nodded. "You hungry?" he asked, heading down the same corridor.

"It depends on what you're offering."

The guy's scowl deepened. "If you like all that crappy veggie stuff, then you're going to love it, but if you were hoping for meat, you're shit out of luck."

"I'm fine with the veggies."

"Good, because that is all Okidu is cooking."

"You have a cook?"

"No, not really."

Andrew waited to hear the rest, but evidently it was all Bhathian was going to say.

Surly son of a bitch.

The guy was built like a pro-wrestler and had the nasty disposition to match. Tall, he was about Kian's height, but probably outweighed Syssi's boyfriend by at least a hundred pounds.

Still, despite his intimidating size and his bushy, dark eyebrows being clenched in what appeared to be a permanent scowl, Bhathian wasn't a bad-looking dude. In fact, the ladies probably found him attractive, particularly those who were into the big, tough, silent types.

"Take a seat." Bhathian motioned to a barstool as they entered the huge, commercial-style kitchen.

There was no dining table per se, only a long stainless steel prep area with several barstools thrown in at one end.

Bhathian pulled out a half-empty pan of lasagna from a warming drawer and a couple of beers from the fridge, and brought the loot to the table, then went back for plates and utensils.

"Dig in," he said after scooping half of the leftover lasagna onto his plate.

As Andrew piled his plate with the rest of it, Bhathian wolfed down several forkfuls, then took a swig from his beer. "So, you're Syssi's brother...," he said.

"Yeah?"

"And you're some kind of commando or Special Ops as they call it today, right?"

"Not anymore, retired. Now I'm a desk jockey. Though still in the same field."

"Retired? At your age?"

Andrew was starting to like the guy. "Too old for active duty."

"Anandur told me he was impressed with your skills, you know, on both missions."

The guy was either trying to make conversation or working up to something.

"Old age has one advantage. It entails a lot of experience."

Bhathian snorted. "Old age... you're forgetting who you're talking to. Compared to me you're an infant."

Now, that was a tad offensive...

"Yeah, well, I do have a lot of experience in particular kinds of situations, which makes me a valuable asset to my government even from behind a desk."

"That you are. You're a valuable asset to us as well." Bhathian rubbed his neck, his eyebrows riding even lower. "I...," he started and stopped, "I need a favor...," he gritted, cupping the back of his almost shaved skull with his huge hand.

Andrew waited for the guy to continue.

Bhathian avoided Andrew's eyes when he spoke. "There is something I've been trying to find for nearly thirty years and reached a dead end at each turn. But you... you might have access to information I don't even know exists."

He sucked half his beer on a oner, then faced Andrew. "I've never told anyone, and whether you can, or will help me or not, I need to know that this will stay between us."

"No problem."

Bhathian's gray eyes were trained on Andrew's for a long moment before he nodded.

CHAPTER 29: SYSSI

"*G*et out of here!" Amanda gasped.

"I know, two weeks, crazy… right?"

"Yeeeee…" All Syssi heard was the yeeping and the swish of wind.

It was easy to picture Amanda pirouetting on deck with the phone in hand.

Apparently, her friend, or rather her future sister-in-law, was cruising down the California coast on a luxury yacht.

The deserter…

"Yeah, I bet it's very exciting to hear about it, but planning a wedding that is supposed to be the most memorable event in the clan's history, not so much. I'm getting an anxiety attack like every five minutes."

"Fear not, Amanda the great to the rescue."

Syssi's shoulders sagged in relief. "Oh, thank you.

You can't imagine how much I appreciate your coming back to help me."

The long stretch of silence had Syssi tense all over again.

"I can't, not yet. But I'm going to work on it from here. We can divide the tasks between the three of us, with you having the last say on all final decisions, of course." Amanda's idea sounded reasonable, but after Syssi had her hopes up, the disappointment stung.

Still, she was being selfish, wasn't she? Amanda needed to be away just as much as Syssi needed her to be back.

On the other hand, this wedding was a once in a lifetime affair, while Amanda could go on her vacation whenever. "Yeah, sure. But it's not the same. I need you here to keep me from falling apart."

Amanda sighed. "Oh, sweetie, I know. I'll try to come back as soon as I can. But I need a little more time."

Syssi chewed on her lower lip, debating if she should bring up the thorny subject. But Amanda needed to know. "Kian is finally going to talk to Dalhu sometime later today, and he asked Andrew to be there when he does."

"That's good... Yeah...," Amanda whispered.

"Talk to me. What's going on with you?" Syssi wanted to kick herself. Obviously, Amanda wasn't in a good place despite the cheerful confidence she was fronting. And all Syssi had been concerned with were her own petty problems and her needs. She hadn't paused to think that maybe it was Amanda who needed her help and not the other way around.

Some friend you are...

And Syssi's problems? What problems? Those were happy problems...

"Hold on...," Amanda said. "Hey, Lana, go scrub some toilets, would you? I want to talk with my bestie without you eavesdropping." She shooed this Lana away.

"Who is Lana?"

"One of Alex's crew of Russian lesbos." Amanda snorted.

Syssi chuckled. "That sounds interesting, Russian lesbians? How would you know?"

"Well, the Russian accents give them away."

"The lesbian part, you witch!"

"I'm just kidding, or maybe not, who knows? It's just that they are so butch. Same short haircut, like really boy short, and muscles that would put most guys to shame. Not to mention a complete lack of manners. Not that their peculiar social graces have anything to do with sexual orientation, it's just the cherry on top of this crew's overall *feminine, ladylike* bearing."

"I see. But if they are so rude, what are you still doing there?"

"I'm curious," Amanda whispered, though this time it wasn't a sad, choked-up whisper, more like conspiratorial. "Tonight, I'm going to get them drunk and find out what's going on." Her whisper was barely audible.

"Good luck with that." Amanda had an impressive capacity for alcohol, but compared to the legendary Russians? She would be drunk way before them.

"Don't worry. I got it."

She probably did. After all, Amanda had some pretty nifty abilities in her bag of tricks. "Are you going to compel them? Or thrall them? Or whatever you call the thing you do?"

"I wish it was that easy. But thralling and influencing work only on unsuspecting, receptive minds. Compelling people to do something they are actively resisting is nearly impossible—except for the really weak minded. And in the case of suspicious, stubborn Russians, I don't think even Yamanu is powerful enough to compel them to spill. But shitloads of vodka might do it."

"Okay, Mata Hari. Now tell me where you're at."

Amanda sighed. "I'm in limbo. I can't stand the sight of Dalhu, knowing he is responsible for Mark's murder, but I can't stand being without him either.

Even the thought of getting it on with some random guy makes me want to retch. So yeah, I'm screwed, and not in a good way."

Yeah, that was one hell of a conundrum. "You must've known he was associated with the murder. It shouldn't have been such a big shock."

"I know. What can I say, I blocked it. And associated is not the same as being the one who ordered it."

Damn. What was she supposed to say to that? What would she do in Amanda's place? Probably the same thing—run as far and as fast as she could.

"Maybe you should talk with your mother. If anyone has a chance to find a way to reconcile this, it is her."

Way to go, Syssi, drop it at someone else's feet.

But she had no words of wisdom to offer.

"I suppose, though I don't think I'm ready to listen to anything one way or the other."

"I understand completely. Remember the night at the club? When Kian came to get me?"

"Yeah?"

"I don't think I've ever told you, but just before he showed up, I was convinced that you guys were mafia and that he was the boss."

"What? Why?"

"Well, what do you think? You and Kri kept taking guys to the back rooms, and after you were done with whatever you were doing there, they just walked away without as much as a wave goodbye. I thought you were selling them drugs. Then Arwel and Bhathian show up, looking like bodyguards, saying that they came to keep an eye on us, but couldn't sit with me because they didn't want to infringe on your turf. Combined with the attack at the lab, the secrecy... you get the picture."

"Oh, wow, totally... So what did you do?"

"I tried to make a run for it, but Alex—who by the way is a total creep—got in my way. I really don't understand how you can be friends with someone like that. Just saying. Then Kian showed up, and I was freaking out because being involved with a mafia boss felt like a death sentence. I was terrified. And yet, when he dragged me onto the dance floor and held me tight, I couldn't help wanting him like crazy. I was so confused. I couldn't understand how I could possibly feel safe in his arms while suspecting he was the worst kind of criminal."

"Fascinating story, and I get what you're trying to say, but it's not the same. There is no denying that Dalhu is a murderer, and Kian isn't really a mafia boss."

"Here is the thing, though, I'm not sure I would have been able to walk away from Kian even if he turned out to be a criminal. And as to Dalhu, if he is a murderer, then every soldier who has ever killed is a murderer too."

After a long pause Amanda responded. "No, Syssi, you are wrong. I wish you weren't, but unfortunately you are. Soldiers fight other soldiers on the battlefield; it is ugly and sad and horrible, but not as horrible as the premeditated, cold-blooded murder of an unarmed man in his own home."

Sadly, Amanda was absolutely right.

CHAPTER 30: SEBASTIAN

*A*fter the swarm of construction workers had left, Sebastian surveyed the job site. The plumbing and electrical in the basement were already in place, and the partition walls for the small rooms —each with its own bathroom—were up and covered in drywall.

The building above was being repainted inside and out, and all the old bathroom fixtures were piled in a huge dumpster outside. Tomorrow, the new fixtures would get delivered and installed, first in the thirty-eight upstairs bathrooms, then once they were ready, in the twenty-one down in the basement.

The only significant change Sebastian had made, besides the basement conversion, was to combine several rooms on the third floor for his own use, adding a luxurious bathroom and a balcony.

In three to four days most of the place would be ready for furniture, except for his suite of rooms, which would take longer to complete.

After all, luxury demanded time and attention to detail.

The speed with which things were being done could have never been achieved legally. The basement, full of rooms without windows, would have never been permitted, and the rest of the work, although not violating city codes, would have raised suspicion.

Not to mention the time and money it would have taken to pull the countless permits or the delays caused by waiting for inspections.

Still, even though the old monastery was isolated, with that many workers and deliveries of building material, there was a good chance some city official would eventually show up at the site.

Not that the inspector would have anything to report after meeting Sebastian.

Thank Mortdh, he possessed a strong thralling gift. Influencing the minds of the over fifty construction workers at the end of each day would've been time-consuming and exhausting otherwise.

It wasn't that he was concerned that they would report to the city officials. The illegal workmen his contacts had supplied could not and would not talk to the authorities. But without him planting a suggestion that they really didn't want to talk about their work, they were bound to gossip to friends and family.

Tom thought Sebastian was being overly cautious, and that it would have sufficed to muddle their memories once the basement was completed, but Sebastian refused to take the chance of the workmen blabbering in the meantime about the underground facility he was building. And anyway, there was the issue of the electric fence, the new massive gate, and the surveillance cameras that were being installed not only all over the facility and its grounds, but also along the road leading up to it.

Sebastian had no doubt that even the lowly workmen had figured out that this kind of security was excessive for an *Interfaith Spiritual Retreat*.

CHAPTER 31: BHATHIAN

"Okay, so here is the story." Bhathian sucked back the rest of his beer and set the empty bottle down.

One beer would not cut it if he were to tell that shameful tale. He got up and came back with two more.

"I see it's going to be a long one." Andrew saluted with his mostly full bottle, a smirk catching one side of his mouth.

Bhathian felt his glower deepen. It was hard enough to get this story out without snide remarks. "You want to listen or not?"

"Sorry, man, I was just making a joke."

"Okay." Bhathian popped the cap off his second beer. "So, thirty-something years ago, on a flight from Edinburgh to LA, the flight attendant I was flirting with invited me to join her for drinks at this little-known bar next to the airport. As it turned out, the place was, still is, a favorite watering hole for many of the transcontinental flights' stewardesses and pilots."

Bhathian took a swig of his beer, then wiped his mouth with the back of his hand. "The place was packed with beautiful women, and due to the nature of its transient clientele, unlike the other bars and clubs, there was a never-ending supply of fresh lovelies."

And the best part? None of the other males in his family had known about it.

He had struck gold.

His private hunting ground.

Andrew saluted with his bottle. "Sweet, my kind of place."

"That's where I met Trish." One of the most beautiful women he had ever met. "Patricia Evans, a first-class flight attendant on the now-defunct TWA."

Bhathian palmed his bottle. "We went back to her hotel room." And she had been incomparable. In more ways than one.

"Trish turned out to be one of those rare mortals who cannot be thralled."

"Not at all? Or just resistant?" Andrew asked.

"I don't know. I'm not great at it, but I had no trouble with anyone before or since. But anyway, luckily, I figured it out before biting her, otherwise… yeah, it would've been one hell of a fuckfest."

"What did you do?"

"What do you think? I didn't bite her. We said our goodbyes, and I thought it was the end of it, that I would never see her again."

It had hurt because for the first time ever Bhathian had wanted more with a woman.

"But you did."

"A month later, she found me at the bar. And I figured, sweet, why not."

Bhathian closed his eyes at the memory, her image still as vivid as it had been thirty years ago. "I didn't get to bite her, but she was so fucking gorgeous—with that banging body of hers, and hair so black it was almost blue, and so long it was kissing the top curve of her perfect ass." He felt his face redden, and he looked away, embarrassed by what he'd said out loud. Too late to take it back, though.

"We went back to her room again, but instead of shucking her clothes, she pulled out one of those miniature whiskey bottles and handed it to me."

"YOU'LL NEED IT," *she told him, a beautiful blush climbing up her cheeks.*

He gulped it and lifted a brow.

"I'm pregnant."

Oh, hell. This was so not what he had been expecting.

"And you think it's mine?"

"I know it is, I've been with no one else for months." Trish didn't look upset. If anything, she seemed to glow with joy.

He hated himself for it, but he said it anyway. *"I want you to abort it. I'll pay whatever expenses and loss of income you'll incur, but there is nothing more I can offer you. I'm sorry."*

Trish looked as if he had slapped her, and in a way, he felt like he had. Though what did she expect? Even if he chose to believe her, and for some reason he did, this pregnancy was the result of a one-night stand, for heaven's sakes.

"I'm not going to abort my child," she whispered.

"Trish, be reasonable. I am not what you need, I can't be. A beautiful woman like you should have no trouble finding a good man. One that will make you happy, be a proper father to your children."

Damn, he would've loved nothing more than a chance to be that man.

"You don't understand, this is a miracle. I'm forty-five, and I haven't been on contraceptives for years because I couldn't get pregnant. And here I am, with a child growing inside me..." Tears began sliding down her cheeks.

"Oh, hell, Trish..." He took her in his arms. *"I didn't*

know..." She was forty-five? She looked no older than thirty, and even that was a stretch.

"It's okay. I didn't come here expecting anything from you, just thought you'd be happy to know that you've created a child... and maybe... maybe put your name on the birth certificate when the time comes..."

Fuck, he couldn't do even that. All he could do was offer money, and although Trish would no doubt hate it, she would need it.

"I'm sorry, I can't do that."

"Oh my God, you're married, aren't you?"

"No, I didn't lie about that... it's just that I have some legal issues." It was kind of true... "But I can give you money, enough so you and your child will never lack anything."

Yes, this was good. He could help support her, and maybe get to watch over her and the kid from afar.

"Thank you, that's very generous of you."

CHAPTER 32: ANDREW

"*D*id she take the money?"

Bhathian closed his eyes and shook his head. "I haven't heard from her since. I kept hoping she'd call, kept going to that bar, but she never came back."

"Did you try to find her?"

"For a time. I got a hold of her employment record, so I had her address and social security number. I also discovered that she quit her job shortly after talking to me. But when I went looking for her at the address she provided, the place was already rented out to someone else. The manager said that she was never there, and he doubted she ever really lived there. The rent money, however, he said, was arriving in the mail like clockwork until about the same time she quit the airline. Other than that, I wasn't able to find anything else. It was like she never existed before applying for the job at TWA, and she vanished after quitting it."

Bhathian rubbed his neck. "Eventually, I gave up and tried not to think about the child I might have somewhere or how Patricia was managing, raising that child by herself. But from time to time I still wonder, you know?"

He cast Andrew a sad look. "When I heard about your connections, I thought maybe you could find out for me—working for the government as you do, and having access to information I wasn't able to get to."

Poor guy. The woman had probably used a fake name and social to get the job and had changed it again after quitting it. It wasn't that unusual. She might have been running from an abusive boyfriend or husband, or maybe even from the law. Or she might've been an illegal immigrant. In any case, it would be next to impossible to pick up a trail that was thirty years old. Especially when all he had to go on were a fake name and social, and an approximate age.

Andrew finished what was left of his beer. "You don't happen to have a picture of her, do you?"

"No."

"If I hook you up with a forensic artist, could you describe her well enough for him to draw one?"

"Yes, though what good would it do? If she is still alive, Patricia would be seventy-five now."

"I know, but that's all we have. A name and social that were probably fake, Patricia's approximate age, and that of her child, and your memory of her."

"Fuck." Bhathian sagged on his barstool and popped the cap off his third beer. "Well, it was worth a shot."

"Do you still have that social?"

"Yeah, and the address as well."

"Good. Don't get your hopes up, but I'm going to look into it. And I'll hook you up with the forensic artist."

"Thank you." Bhathian offered his hand.

Andrew shook on it and clapped the guy's shoulder. "No problem."

Damn, the thing was like solid rock—muscles on top of muscles.

Bhathian shifted in his seat, then pushed to his feet. "I'm going to see what's keeping Kian." With his head hung low, he pivoted on his heel and strode away.

By the looks of him, the guy wasn't used to talking about himself, and confiding in another—especially a mortal—must've rankled.

Andrew shook his head as he tried to put himself in the guy's shoes.

To know that he had a son or a daughter that he'd

never gotten to see, never gotten to support, to protect, must've festered inside Bhathian for the past thirty years.

But then, it would've been the same for any decent human being—or immortal.

Kian walked into the kitchen. "Thank you for coming, Andrew. Sorry that I kept you waiting." He offered his hand.

Apparently, Bhathian's escort duty was finished.

"No problem, Bhathian took good care of me." Andrew motioned to the empty lasagna pan and the lineup of beer bottles.

"Good. You ready to go?" Kian waited for Andrew to get up, and together they headed out.

"Any instructions before we talk to the Doomer?" Andrew asked.

"I trust your judgment. Mostly, I want you there to detect his lies. But feel free to ask the Doomer questions if you feel like I'm overlooking something."

"If I catch him lying, do you want me to tell you later or give you a sign right away? I'd rather not say anything about it. It's better if he doesn't know I can do this."

They stopped in front of the elevator, and Kian punched the down button. "I want to know right away. How about tapping your shoe? Or clearing your throat? I don't want to chance missing a visual cue."

"When he lies, I'll tap my shoe twice."

Kian gave a nod, and as the elevator door opened with a ping, they got inside, then exited a few seconds later—four levels below.

Down the corridor, Anandur was leaning against the wall next to one of the doors with his arms crossed over his chest.

Andrew slanted a look at Kian. "You think we need him there? Between the two of us, I'm sure we can handle one prisoner."

The guy grimaced. "Standard protocol. As Regent, I'm supposed to have a bodyguard at all times. I get away with not always following it, but in this case, Anandur insisted."

"Aren't you the one making the rules?"

"Nope. This one was Annani's doing. And as such, it is set in stone."

"I see." Andrew chuckled.

As he had already figured, the Goddess had the ultimate say.

Tough little lady.

"Good evening, gentlemen, ready to proceed?" Anandur punched the security code into the keypad, and the door began its inward swing.

"After you." Kian motioned for Andrew to enter.

The Doomer was sitting on the couch with his

palms down on his thighs, his nonthreatening pose belied by the way he was eyeing them with thinly veiled hostility.

But the Doomer had nothing on Kian.

The guy's hands curled into tight fists, and his eyes began their eerie glow.

Andrew put a hand on Kian's tight shoulder. "Easy, my man," he whispered, warily watching Kian's lips for those monstrous fangs to make an appearance.

With an apparent effort, Kian uncurled his fists and walked over to the bar. "Scotch, anyone?" When no one answered, he poured himself a glass and downed it on a oner, then poured another before sitting down in an armchair across from the Doomer.

Anandur walked over to the small dining table near the bar and planted his butt in a chair.

As Andrew sat next to Kian in the other armchair, he took a quick look around. The room was a far cry from the prison cell he had imagined. In fact, it was a lot fancier than his own living room, and through the open door he glimpsed an adjoining bedroom as luxurious as any high-end hotel's.

Complete with a large screen television and a game console, the Doomer's accommodations were fit for a king. He had no reason to look so pissed off.

"Where is Amanda? What have you done with her?" the Doomer bit out.

Aha, so that's why...

Andrew wasn't even aware Amanda was gone. Had Kian sent her away? Or what was more likely, she was still here but had smartened up enough to stay away from Dalhu.

"None of your damn business. But I don't mind telling you that she left of her own volition, not because I forced her to. She finally woke up and realized what a piece of shit you are and doesn't want to see you."

The Doomer could not have looked worse if Kian had shot him. He closed his eyes and slumped back into the couch cushions.

Andrew actually felt pity for the bastard. There was nothing worse than shattered hopes.

"I'm going to ask you some questions," Kian said.

"Why should I tell you anything." It was more of a statement than a question.

And it wasn't about defiance either.

The Doomer simply didn't seem to care about anything. Which wasn't going to do them any good. He had to give the guy something to hold on to.

Leaning forward, Andrew peered into Dalhu's dark eyes. "Because even if Amanda never wants to see you again, you still want to make sure she is safe."

Dalhu sighed and shifted up. "You're right, even if it's the last thing I do."

From the corner of his eye, Andrew caught Kian looking down at the shoe he hadn't tapped, and a smirk tugged at his mouth.

The Doomer hadn't lied, though, he'd meant what he'd said.

"Did you take out my men?"

"It was all taken care of," Kian said in a surprisingly conversational tone.

Was he mellowing out toward the Doomer?

"Good. She can return to her work now. She loves it..." Dalhu's voice petered out to a near whisper at the end.

It had the opposite effect on Kian. "Tell me about the incoming reinforcements and what is their plan of action," he barked.

In the silence that followed, the Doomer's internal conflict was barely perceptible on his hard face, but in the end, his eyes narrowed on Kian as he decided to speak his piece. "I don't give a fuck if you believe me or not, but just for the record... the set of rules I'd been operating under before meeting Amanda no longer applies."

"Noted," Kian bit out.

Dalhu nodded. "I wasn't told how many are coming, but if I were to guess, at least fifty, but no more than a hundred. And with a contingent this big, someone higher up on the chain of command will be leading them."

Andrew pulled out his phone and began recording, even though he had no doubt he could later retrieve everything from security. But having his own would save him a trip, not to mention having to deal with whatever paperwork was required to obtain copies. "Can you make a list of probable candidates for the leader position? There shouldn't be too many at that level."

"Probably, but what good will it do?"

"The names alone, none. But compiling a file for each of the top players in the game, including a physical description, a set of attributes, a style of command, and any other information you can think of is a critical first step."

Kian cast Andrew an approving look. "You really know your shit, don't you?"

"This is elementary. Information is the most valuable asset there is, and you should always gather as much of it as you can about your adversaries, as well as your allies. True?"

"True," the Doomer agreed. "Give me a pen and some paper, and I'll give it my best shot."

Kian again glanced at Andrew's motionless foot before returning his eyes to the Doomer. "I'll do better than that, I'll give you a laptop."

"A laptop will be great, but I still need a pen and

paper if you want me to sketch their portraits for you."

Andrew snorted. "No offense to your doodling skill, my man, but I'd rather have you describe them to a forensic artist."

The Doomer seemed more amused than offended. "Anyone have a piece of paper and a pen?"

"I think I have something." Anandur pushed to his feet and pulled out a folded green piece of paper from his back pocket, then straightened what turned out to be some sort of flyer and handed it to Dalhu. "You can use the back."

Andrew rolled his eyes but produced a pen from his jacket's inside pocket. "Here, knock yourself out."

Dalhu placed the flyer face down on the coffee table and ran his hand over it a couple of times to smooth out the creases, then went to work.

Anandur crouched next to him, while Kian and Andrew leaned forward, all three observing the image Dalhu's fast pen strokes were creating.

"I'll be damned." Anandur was the first to say something as Amanda's face took shape on paper, and Andrew was tempted to echo the sentiment.

It was brilliant, and not only because the depiction was strikingly true. Amanda's spirit—her playful haughtiness, the stubborn tilt of her chin, the shadow of old pain in her eyes—it was all there, black pen strokes on green paper as if the Doomer had glimpsed her soul.

"What? Did I get something wrong?" Dalhu voice was hesitant as he lifted his head to look at Anandur.

"No, nothing. This is fucking amazing." Anandur took the sketch and handed it to Kian. "Take a look at this."

Kian looked at it for a long moment, then handed it back to Dalhu. "Very good. You proved your point. You've got talent."

The guy had proved his point and then some, and Andrew wasn't referring to the Doomer's sketching skill.

Dalhu swallowed. "It's nothing, just a good visual memory and attention to detail, that's all. Useful..." His body began swelling with aggression as his eyes darted between them.

The guy acted as if he had been caught wearing lipstick or ladies' undergarments. Evidently, in Dalhu's camp, artistic ability was not considered as befitting a fighter.

"I sing." Anandur caught on fast. "And I'm damn good." He began a merry tune in what sounded like Old Norse, and by the sparkle in his eyes and expressive hand gestures was about the female form.

He had a good, deep, rumbling voice that only enhanced his masculinity. It wasn't helping.

Well, what the hell. Andrew joined the effort.

"Unfortunately, I have no special talent, but I wish I did."

Kian regarded them as if they were idiots. "What these two are trying to say is that your talent is a gift, not something to hide and be embarrassed about. Not here, and not even for a warrior."

Dalhu shrugged. "If you say so, I've never looked at it as anything other than a useful tool."

Anandur clapped the Doomer's back. "I'm no expert, but this is good."

"Enough about that." Kian waved at Anandur to go back to his seat. "I'll get you a laptop and some sketching supplies. Now tell me about the plan."

CHAPTER 33: DALHU

For a moment, Dalhu contemplated playing down his part.

But it seemed he had gained some ground with Kian; the waves of hatred the guy had been emitting had subsided, if only marginally. It would be lost once Dalhu admitted to being the mastermind behind this new threat to Kian's family. Except, Dalhu had already admitted everything to the Goddess, and even the slightest subterfuge would undermine his credibility.

And besides, he didn't really care what Kian or the rest of them thought of him. The only one whose opinion he valued had already decided he wasn't worthy.

And yet, even though he knew it to be the honest truth, so had Amanda when she had accepted him before. She'd had no illusions as to who and what he was. So why the change of heart? What had made her flee without even giving him the courtesy of a see-you-in-hell goodbye?

Maybe Kian had lied. Maybe he'd found out about her visit and had made sure it wouldn't happen again.

Yes, that was the only thing that made sense. And if this was indeed the case, all was not lost.

Amanda would find a way.

As he felt the dark cloud of despair lift, Dalhu fought hard to keep his expression impassive. No reason to tip his hand and let Kian suspect he was on to him.

"Start from the beginning. From what you and your team were sent to do and why, to the reason you asked for reinforcements, and what they are planning to do," Andrew clarified.

At first, Dalhu hadn't understood what use the clan could possibly have for a mortal. But he was starting to realize that the guy was a valuable asset. Andrew seemed to know what he was doing and was levelheaded, methodical and thorough—unlike the hot-headed Kian.

Dalhu nodded. "It was retaliation for that computer virus you helped your allies develop. I was to find the team of programmers that made it happen and take out the best one. It was supposed to send you a message; you mess with ours, we will mess with yours. Nothing new there."

"How did you find them?" Andrew asked, and Dalhu noticed just then that the guy was recording everything on his phone.

Smart.

"We had an informant. Not in the programming unit, but somewhere higher up in the defense department. I can't give you a name, though, or even a description, because I never dealt with the guy. The info went to my superior first, and he passed it down to me."

Andrew's brows furrowed. "You guys managed to bribe someone high ranking in the defense department? These people have to go through an extensive vetting process, and I'm sure their finances are closely monitored."

Dalhu shrugged. "I wasn't privy to that kind of information. I was just a field commander of a small unit. But from what I've gathered over the years, there are several ways the Brotherhood goes about it. The best is to raise a mole from the ground up. The Brotherhood recruits promising young boys, who are then brainwashed into supporting whatever cause they invent for them. The recruiters then help them and their families in ways that are hard to detect—ensuring the parents get well-paying jobs, and the boys and their siblings get scholarships to the best universities. Then the Brotherhood waits patiently for them to climb up the ranks. Eventually, a few of the many that were nurtured make it to critical positions."

Andrew whistled. "That's a very long-term approach. Makes sense, though. Time considerations are different for immortals."

Kian got up to refill his glass. "And the other methods?"

"The run-of-the-mill bribes and blackmails."

"Go on. So what happened next?" Kian asked.

Damn, now was the part Dalhu was dreading. "We had the name of the civilian programming unit —the one masquerading as a gaming company—but their offices had the kind of security we had no chance of breaching. And we had no idea who their top programmer was. So we surveyed the building and followed them around for a couple of days. Until one evening, they all went to celebrate at a bar. From there it was easy. Pinpointing the one they were all saluting, following him home, and taking him out."

As Dalhu cast a longing look at Kian's drink, he couldn't help but notice the guy's fingers tightening around the glass. Any moment, the thing would shatter in his hand.

"And no one stopped to question him before killing him? You had an untrained male from your enemy's clan. Why waste such a rare opportunity?" Andrew asked.

"We didn't know he was one of yours. And the guy sent after him had his orders. Fortunately for you, Doomers don't question their orders. Otherwise, your location would have been already compromised."

Although true, he regretted his choice of words. To use the word fortunate in this context had been a mistake. Except, he wasn't a diplomat, and his mastery of the English language didn't include a rich vocabulary.

Judging by the baleful expression on Kian's face, Dalhu wouldn't live long enough to expand it either.

"Indeed." Andrew cast a somber glance at Kian. "I'm sorry for your loss, Kian, but at least the man hadn't been tortured. True?" He pinned Dalhu with a hard stare.

"Just fangs and venom." Dalhu glanced briefly at Kian and felt a pang of guilt.

And envy.

Kian, the leader of Annani's clan, wasn't just angry about losing a great programmer, he was mourning the guy's death. In contrast, no one ever gave a damn about a Doomer's demise.

No one would mourn Dalhu.

Still, the fact was that the clan got more than

even. "You took out eleven of mine and have me down here. I think your loss has been avenged."

Damn, it was again the wrong thing to say. Kian looked ready to tear out his throat. "Just do yourself a favor, Doomer, and don't try to equate the two. Clear?" he hissed through his fangs.

As much as Dalhu hated the supercilious jerk, Kian was right. It wasn't the same. Unlike Dalhu and his men, the programmer had not been a fighter. Dalhu bowed his head. "My apologies, you are right."

That seemed to somewhat mollify the guy, and the dangerous glow in his eyes subsided. "How did you know where to find Amanda, though?"

"My men found a framed article about Amanda's research, with a personal dedication from her to the programmer. When they brought it back to me, I had a hunch she was related to the guy and decided to check it out. The presence of Guardians at her lab confirmed my suspicion. But running into her that day on the street was purely coincidental."

A very lucky, fated coincidence.

Kian's face hardened. "How did you know it was her? Did you sense she was an immortal?"

"No, of course not. There is no way to detect immortal females." Dalhu paused as he remembered that he had been compelled to follow Amanda even before recognizing her. "To tell you the truth, I'm not sure. I knew her face from the picture in the article, but I felt the urge to go after her even though all I saw was her retreating back. And not only because she is exquisite from any angle."

The mortal eyed him with open curiosity. "What made you run and leave everything you knew behind, instead of delivering her to your leader?"

"First of all, I would have never handed over an immortal female to my brethren. Second, would you have done differently?"

The guy chuckled. "Good point. Though I'm not in the habit of abducting women when they refuse to come willingly."

Yeah, the human probably had no trouble finding willing candidates for his affections. Still... "You also have no shortage of possible mates. There are probably millions of them in this city alone. I, on the other hand, had this one and only chance, and I was not going to let it get away, even if it went against my own code of honor."

"Wasn't aware Doomers had any," Kian gritted.

"First of all, I'm no longer a Doomer. And second, honor is subjective. And even those who others consider monsters sometimes cling to their own notion of honor."

Kian wasn't impressed. "Good, I see you have no illusions as to what you are."

The condescending prick.

"I might be a monster, but I would have never

treated my own sister the way you did yours. No matter what."

As Dalhu's barb hit home, Kian's wince was deeply satisfying.

"We are getting off track here, guys." Andrew raised his palm to halt Kian's retort. "So what happened next?"

Dalhu rubbed his neck. "After the first team encountered Guardians at Amanda's lab, the same night I sent another to search it for clues. They found her journal, which I learned a lot from."

Kian snorted. "Yeah, like the names of her top test subjects, which you tried to snatch."

"Yes. But also that you guys adhere to the old taboo against in-line mating, and with no Dormants of other lines, are all the descendants of one female. Which finally explained your age-old tactic of hiding instead of facing the Brotherhood head-on. There just aren't enough of you."

"So, you decided it wouldn't be all that difficult to hunt us into extinction." The hatred wafting off of Kian was not only pungent but felt like a tangible force—pervasive and oppressive.

Not that Dalhu could fault the guy. He sighed. "Actually, my first response was a grudging respect. Achieving all that you had with so few members is damn impressive."

Kian shifted in his chair. "Glad you approve," he hissed.

"Not at all. In my opinion, you're wasting your efforts. Mortals are not worth it. Their herd mentality is ill-suited for democracy. They're better off being led and controlled. But this is neither here nor there. Anyway, after being bested by your Guardians time and again, I did some thinking and figured that their presence indicated a clan stronghold somewhere around LA. But to find it I didn't need to catch a Guardian. Any immortal would do. And where better to hunt for immortal males than the places they frequent hunting for hookups—bars and clubs. But as there are hundreds of those in this city, I needed more men to conduct an adequate search."

Andrew frowned. "But from what you've said before, your superiors were not sending you more men to command, but replacing you with a higher ranking officer."

CHAPTER 34: KIAN

The Doomer chuckled. "I knew they wouldn't leave such an important mission to me, but I hoped to get credit for the idea, maybe even a larger and better-trained unit under my command."

Kian didn't know if he hated the guy more or less for his dispassionate recounting, or for being so absolutely, fucking honest. Andrew's foot hadn't tapped even once, and he'd been watching the thing like a hawk.

Plotting the demise of Kian's family had been just a job for the Doomer, an assignment, an opportunity for advancement. The guy was a cold, opportunistic bastard, nothing more.

What the hell did Amanda see in that thing?

And yet, the Doomer wasn't cold when it came to

her. That sketch, more than anything he might have said, proved that the guy not only had feelings for Amanda, but had somehow gotten to know her pretty damn well in the short time he'd had her. And not only in the biblical sense.

And what's worse, Kian had to admit, if grudgingly, that a soulless creature couldn't have imbued his rendering of Amanda with so much life, emotion, and insight.

Andrew touched his phone to stop the recording and got up. "I'm ready for a drink. What can I get you, Dalhu?"

The Doomer looked grateful. "Whatever you're having."

Andrew glanced at Kian. "A refill?"

"Yeah." He got up and handed Andrew his empty glass.

What an asset the guy was turning out to be. How had he managed all this time without him? Andrew practically took over the interrogation and was doing a much better job than Kian would have done.

Evidently, there was something to be said for emotional distance—or maybe proper training.

Dalhu drained his glass, and Andrew poured him another before going back to his chair.

"Okay, let's move on to your fascinating home

base." Andrew touched his phone's screen to restart the recording.

"I assume the Goddess has told you what I've told her."

"Yes, we know about the Brotherhood's underground facility, and the world-class brothel your leader runs on the other side of that island. From what I understood, the security is extremely tight, but I want to hear more. Everything from facts to suspicions to guesses. No place is airtight. There must be a way to infiltrate the island."

With Andrew conducting the questioning, Kian leaned back in his chair, not at all minding being relegated to the role of a passive observer.

As far as he was concerned, there was nothing to be gained from this line of questioning anyway.

He wasn't planning on storming his enemy stronghold, no matter how much he despised Doomers, or how much he pitied the enslaved females—mortal and Dormant alike. It just wasn't feasible, and Kian wasn't in the habit of indulging in make-believe scenarios.

"A single human may have a chance, but not an immortal." Dalhu looked at Andrew. "The immortal guards would sniff another immortal right away. He wouldn't get through the first line of security. And although the only way to get in, which is even remotely conceivable, would be as a client, I have no idea how one would go about getting an invitation or even being in the know."

"Who are the typical customers?"

"The rich, powerful and corrupt. From all over the world."

"That doesn't tell me much, could you be more specific?"

"It's not as if I went around asking questions and mingling with the guests. But the girls aren't required to be as tight-lipped with the soldiers as they are with the other clients, and they like nothing more than a piece of juicy gossip. Then again, it's not like the johns introduce themselves by name and title. From what I've garnered, though, they are a diversified crowd; drug lords, arms dealers, oil tycoons, officers of large corporations, politicians, judges, professors, and even the occasional royal."

Andrew frowned. "I bet that it isn't only money your leader collects from his distinguished clientele. Information and favors most likely bring an even greater profit."

No doubt.

Kian was starting to wonder if he hadn't deluded himself over the years, thinking the clan had at least a financial advantage over the Doomers. From what Dalhu was telling them, it seemed Navuh created his own fountain of gold.

But again, although enlightening, the information was useless. "Where are you going with this, Andrew? It's not like we can do anything about it. Even if we can get a mortal in there, what could one guy do?"

"Information, as I've said before, is priceless. And you need as much of it as you can get because you never know when it will become handy. Knowing who the Brotherhood has in its pockets is in itself vital. And even if we can't do anything to help the women already trapped there, maybe we can do something about the supply end of it."

Apparently, there was such a thing as an information addiction, and Andrew had it bad. "I'm sorry, Andrew, but from where I stand, the risk is not worth the potential gain. To me anyway. Our clan is not the government."

Andrew's brows drew tight. "I'm not sure you're right about that. I'll collect what I can from Dalhu and analyze it." He smiled. "You know I would love to sink my teeth into this."

Okay, the guy is both information and adrenaline junkie. "Even if I were willing to risk you on a suicide mission like this, which I'm not, your sister would kill me if I did. So when you think of a plan, don't include yourself in it. Not going to happen."

Andrew pinned him with a hard stare. "Syssi wasn't privy to my missions before, and she is not going to be in the future. And last I checked, I'm not working for you, and you have no authority over me."

"Ahem." Anandur cleared his throat.

Damn. Kian really liked the guy, but Andrew was a pain in the ass—with an iron will and no respect for authority.

Still, he was right about the independent agent status, and it was something Kian intended to remedy as soon as possible. If putting the guy on payroll was going to make him more manageable, Kian would hire him in a heartbeat. "We will discuss this later."

Andrew nodded and turned back to the Doomer.

And what do you know, it was the first time Kian had seen Dalhu smiling.

"Wipe that smirk off your face," Kian barked at him. "And you too." He pointed a finger at Anandur.

"Yes, sir." Anandur saluted and turned his face to the wall, but his heaving shoulders betrayed him.

The Doomer had his head bowed down as if concentrating real hard on the scuff on his boot.

Damn, what did a guy have to do to get some respect...

Three hours, God knows how many drinks, and a platter of munchies later, Andrew was finally satisfied that he'd squeezed out of Dalhu all there was to squeeze.

To follow were the profiles of the top players in Navuh's camp, and a map of the island, or rather the parts Dalhu was familiar with.

Not that an infiltration seemed likely.

Unfortunately, Andrew had to agree with Kian. Aside from a spying solo mission, gathering information of a doubtful strategic value, there wasn't much to be gained considering what he'd be risking. Like his head.

Still, he was itching to go.

It was dangerous, and finding who he could blackmail into getting him on the guest list might prove difficult if not impossible. But the idea filled him with renewed vigor and excitement the likes of which he hadn't felt in a long time.

He craved adventure, and Amanda's rescue hadn't even come close to providing enough of a challenge to sate it.

The need to get back the vitality that he felt was leaching out of him at his desk job grabbed him so hard, it overshadowed what he had believed was his quest for Amanda's affections, making a mockery out of it.

Given a choice, he would take the mission and dump Amanda in Dalhu's lap, wishing them the best of luck with a big smile on his face.

And wasn't that a revelation.

Yeah, she was beyond gorgeous, and hot. And competing for her with another man had been a challenge, which he had to admit was part of the lure. But she had not touched his soul the way she had obviously touched Dalhu's. So, even though he still believed himself to be a far better choice for Amanda than the Doomer, and even though with time a deeper connection might've been forged between them, he would be deceiving her and himself if he pretended she had won his heart.

Perhaps she was better off with a lesser man, yet one who loved her with everything he had.

But then, there was Kian.

A big, stubborn obstacle in both Andrew and Amanda's way.

During the long hours of questioning, Kian's attitude toward Dalhu had improved somewhat, and a couple of times he'd even addressed the guy by name instead of spitting the derogative *Doomer*. Yet to hope that he would come around and allow anything between Amanda and Dalhu was ludicrous.

And unless Andrew could come up with a very convincing rationale behind his quest to infiltrate Passion Island, that wasn't going to happen either.

He would most definitely be facing an uphill battle, and so would Amanda if she was still interested in Dalhu.

Though if she was, Andrew doubted even Kian would be able to keep her away from what she wanted. Blood would spill, and Annani would have to put her little, yet formidable foot down to keep her children from tearing each other's throats out.

On a more positive note, Kian had invited Andrew to stop by tomorrow to discuss the possibility of Andrew's inclusion in the clan's organization. Kian had also instructed Anandur to take Andrew to William, where he'd been given a transmitter to install in his car that would allow him access to the clan's underground parking, and his thumbprint had been taken and encoded into the reader of the clan's private elevators.

So progress had been made—he'd been officially accepted into their inner circle—as evidenced by the fact that he was strolling down the corridor of the basement's top level, unescorted, on his way to the clinic.

Now that he'd decided not to pursue Amanda, nothing prevented Andrew from visiting the lovely Dr. Bridget and letting her give him a checkup, or check him out, or anything else she'd had in mind when she'd invited him the other night to stop by.

In fact, Andrew felt quite proud of himself. Bowing out from the competition was the right thing to do.

He wished Amanda good luck.

Though not a religious man by any stretch of the imagination, he felt like offering her a blessing to echo his own epiphany. *May you find the wisdom to realize your heart's desire, the strength to acknowledge it, and the courage to pursue it.*

The end...for now

AMANDA'S STORY CONCLUDES IN
<u>DARK ENEMY REDEEMED</u>

Available on Amazon

TURN THE PAGE FOR AN EXCERPT
DARK ENEMY REDEEMED

DEAR READER,

Thank you for reading the **Children of the Gods**. If you enjoyed the story, I would be grateful if you could leave a short review on Amazon.

With a few words, you'll make me very happy.

Click here to leave a review

Love & happy reading,
Isabell

DARK ENEMY REDEEMED
Book 3 In Amanda & Dalhu's Story

Amanda suspects that something fishy is going on onboard the Anna. But when her investigation of the peculiar all-female Russian crew fails to uncover anything other than more speculation, she decides it's time to stop playing detective and face her real problem—a man she shouldn't want but can't live without.

EXCERPT

"Are you sure? Not a single karaoke machine?"

Freaking Lana probably hadn't bothered to even look for it.

"*Niet*, I found one in a bar, but the owner not want to sell."

"How much did you offer?"

"Two thousand."

"You should've offered more."

"We buy the vodka and the fish you want, and this was all the money left from what you give me."

While the *Anna* moored for the night in Avalon harbor, Amanda had sent Lana and Sonia with instructions to buy supplies and find a karaoke—

whatever the cost. Because c'mon, a party wasn't a party without one.

Especially since this one would be missing the most important element—hunky guys.

Regrettably, though, twenty-three hundred and some change in cash had been all she'd had on her, and the Russians had refused to take her credit card.

The obvious solution would've been to go with them, but she preferred to stay on board—not only because their company was such a dubious pleasure, but because she dreaded encountering horny males and their lustful, leering looks.

Which was sure to happen if she were to grace the streets of Avalon.

There was a price to be paid for beauty, and enduring leering glances from men wasn't even the worst of it—heck, most of the time she didn't mind.

Topping the list were the resentful looks from other females, followed closely by the presumption that all beautiful women were airheads.

Come to think of it, most people, males and females alike, found her looks intimidating.

So yeah, she had been enduring leering glances since she was scarcely a pubescent girl, but they hadn't bothered her before—on the contrary, most times she'd found them arousing.

But nothing was as it used to be.

She was horny, but at the same time felt nauseated by the prospect of a meaningless hookup. And earlier, during her afternoon *nap*, when she'd given self-pleasuring a halfhearted try, it had been more of the same.

Because there was only one male she was able to fantasize about, but the guilt and loathing associated with her attraction to Dalhu weren't exactly conducive to that particular activity.

Shit. It was hell, and it seemed she was going to be stuck in this purgatory for the foreseeable future.

Oh, well, there was nothing to be done about it, except giving it time.

Besides, as the *Anna* swayed gently on the pull and ebb of the tide, lying on a lounger on her top deck wasn't exactly a torment. And the fishy, salty smell of the murky waters wasn't all that bad either. Actually, it could have been quite pleasant if not for the diesel fumes wafting up from the boat's engines.

Fates, how she missed the era of old-fashioned sailboats. The experience had been completely different—the ocean had smelled wonderful —unpolluted.

On the other hand, there was something to be said for the speed, luxury, and modern amenities of the *Anna*.

This was the thing about life—nothing was ever perfect, and to gain one thing you often had to sacrifice another.

And wasn't that the inconvenient truth.

She'd found spending the day with a good book relaxing, and would've loved to keep on reading, but the sun was getting low on the horizon, and even though the drop in temperature wasn't all that significant, it was getting too chilly for lounging in a string bikini.

With a sigh, Amanda closed her book and padded inside.

Back in her cabin, she eyed her laptop. Maybe she should check her e-mail to see if the design ideas for Syssi's wedding gown were ready.

Joann had been amazing, as always, and had contacted all of her designer friends, asking if they'd be willing to do a rush job. But with less than two weeks from idea to final fitting, only two had accepted the challenge of creating an original, breathtaking masterpiece for Amanda's best girl.

Nothing less than spectacular would do for Syssi.

With a frown, Amanda wondered if anyone remembered Kian. After all, the groom also needed something new and fabulous for the event. Unless her brother was planning on showing up at the altar in his fancy Regent robe.

Yeah, right, she chuckled. In her opinion, he looked dashing in it, regal, but she was well aware that Kian detested the thing.

Maybe she should call him and suggest the robe.

At first, Kian would blow up, but then he'd realize it was a joke and they would have a good laugh about it.

Or maybe not.

Amanda plopped down on the king-sized bed and crossed her arms over her eyes. She was dimly aware that the suntan oil she was covered with would leave a sticky imprint on the sheets, but she just didn't give a damn.

Who cared about bed linens when she was contemplating the depressing prospect of never regaining the easygoing, loving relationship she and Kian had enjoyed prior to this whole ugly mess.

Her hand reached for the phone, and she was tempted to hit his number.

But what would she say to him? Ask for his forgiveness?

If she believed it would mend things between them, she would've done it in a heartbeat. Pride, or who was right and who was wrong, was of no consequence when the stakes were so high.

Amanda just wanted her brother back.

Instead, she selected Syssi's number.

"Just a sec"—Syssi answered after the first ring —"let me get someone off the other line."

"Take your time."

Syssi came back after a few moments, puffing as if she'd been running. "I'm all yours."

"What's going on? You sound harried."

"You think? You try planning a wedding for six hundred guests. Neither your mother nor I have any experience in organizing events. And before you ask, no wedding coordinator worth her salt will take the job on such short notice. Ugh, it's going to be a disaster."

Amanda smiled. "Who's the drama queen now? Relax, it's going to be amazing. It shouldn't be all that difficult to arrange for good food, lively music, tasteful decorations, and most importantly—a gorgeous wedding dress."

"Yeah? The way things are going it seems Okidu will have to cook, decorate, and sew the dress. Because every caterer and florist I've called has practically laughed in my face. I had no idea these people are booked months in advance—some even years."

"This is actually a splendid idea. Between Okidu and Onidu and my mother's two, the Odus will have no problem pulling it off. All you need to do is give them a menu, including the recipes, show them pictures of how you want it to look, and they will take it from there."

"You must be kidding, right?"

"I'm dead serious. They can do all of it, except for the dress, which I got covered."

"Oh, yeah? Do tell."

"Hold on, I'm checking my e-mail. Joann, bless

her soul, found not one, but two designers who were willing to take on the challenge, and I'm waiting for the initial sketches." She quickly scrolled through her inbox, but there was nothing from Joann. "Nope... nothing yet. As soon as I have something, I'll forward it to you."

"That's wonderful, thank you. Joann has impeccable taste, I trust her completely."

"Good, I was afraid you'd hate me for not checking with you before talking to her."

"Nah, after outfitting me with an entire wardrobe of fabulous, I trust her to come up with something I can't even imagine. I'm all for letting the pros do their thing. One less item to worry about."

"Poor Syssi, you sound as excited about this wedding as if it was somebody else's."

"I know, right? I hate big events, and being at the center of one is my personal idea of hell. If it were up to me, it would've been just Kian and me, you, Andrew, and Annani. That's it."

"Really? What about your parents? And my sisters Sari and Alena? And the Guardians? And William and Bridget?"

"Okay, them too, but that's it, no one else."

"Oh, sweetie, don't you see? You might be happy with only our immediate families and the few people you know and care for witnessing your joining, but

Kian wants, needs, each and every member of the clan to be there."

"I know. That's why I'm still here and not running off screaming." Syssi let out a huff.

"By the way, speaking of Kian, did anyone remember to get him fitted for a tux for the wedding? If you leave it up to him, he'll show up wearing one of his old business suits."

"You're right, God, I can't believe I didn't think of it." Syssi heaved a sigh. "Just another reminder of how little I know about the man I'm going to marry in thirteen days."

"You know everything that really matters, and you have endless time to learn the rest. So, stop fretting. Kian is a great guy—bad temper and all."

"Yeah, I know... but speaking of your brother's *sunny* disposition," Syssi switched to a whisper, "Kian spent the entire evening with Dalhu and came back... well, I wouldn't say happy, but not enraged either. I think it's an encouraging sign."

Amanda chuckled. "I guess it is—by Kian's standards. Did you ask him what they talked about?" She wasn't curious, not at all...

"He gave me no chance, planting one hot kiss on my mouth and heading straight to his office to grab a file for his next meeting. But I'll grill him later tonight and report to you tomorrow."

In spite of herself, Amanda felt her heart give a

little flutter. Kian must've been in at least a decent mood if the first thing he had done after spending hours with Dalhu was to kiss Syssi.

"Deal. First thing in the morning."

"Are you sure you want me to call you that early? You might be too hungover to talk after your drinking party with the Russians."

"Oh, please, I'll be fine. I'll have them drunk and singing in more ways than one before I'm even tipsy."

Syssi snorted. "If you say so."

"I've got it covered."

Well, almost. Without the karaoke, she would have to make a playlist on her phone and hook it up to the sound system in the grand salon, then hand out printouts of the lyrics to the girls.

Russian songs would have been the best, but unfortunately, although she spoke it with decent fluency, Amanda never bothered to learn to read the Cyrillic script—and mastering it in a span of a couple of hours was a feat that even she couldn't pull off.

As Andrew knocked on the clinic's door, it crossed his mind that it was late and chances were that Dr. Bridget had already gone home.

Disappointed, he gave it one last go and knocked again, then waited. After all, he was already there, and it wasn't as if there was somewhere else he needed to be.

Calling it a night and heading back to his empty house was no more appealing than standing in this deserted corridor and waiting for a woman that might not even be there to let him in.

Kind of pathetic.

The life of a bachelor was not everything the married guys believed it to be.

True, he was free to shag whomever he was able to seduce—and there was no shortage of those—but most nights it just meant that he ended up going home alone.

That's why Syssi's news about the wedding hadn't been such a big surprise—not for him anyway —he'd been expecting it. Though maybe not so soon. He could empathize with Kian's desire to end his lonely bachelor life the moment he'd found the right woman to spend eternity with.

Andrew couldn't even imagine what it must have been like for the guy, spending endless years without someone to share his life with.

He was happy for them, he really was, but he couldn't help feeling a little jealous—even though his single status wasn't anybody's fault but his. And the excuse of his chosen occupation precluding meaningful relationships was just that—an excuse. Somehow it hadn't stopped his comrades from tying the knot.

Problem was, he'd never dated a woman he could imagine spending his life with, and not because none was good enough. Andrew suspected that the flaw was within him—he was either emotionally stunted or just too picky.

Another minute passed, and he was about to turn on his heel and head back when the door finally opened to reveal a surprised Dr. Bridget—the red handbag clutched under her arm betokening that she was on her way out.

Wow! Can you say sexy?

Gone was the conservative doctor, and the woman that had taken her place was hot. Bridget looked ready for action—with her wavy red hair loose around her shoulders and her curvy figure encased in a pair of skin-tight jeans and a clingy red T-shirt. But what had really done it for him were the red, fuck-me heels.

Evidently, Bridget loved to flaunt her red.

Trying hard to look into her pretty eyes and not glance down to peer at her ample cleavage, Andrew ran his hand over his mouth. Who could've guessed the petite physician had been hiding all of this under her doctor's coat?

"I'm sorry, I should have realized it was late. I'll stop by some other time, earlier in the day."

Her eyes widened, and she grabbed his hand, giving a strong tug. "Nonsense, you are coming with me." She pulled him behind her as she went inside and flipped the lights back on. There was a sly little smile on her lovely face as she turned around and looked up. "I'm not going to waste the opportunity of you coming to see me of your own volition. I thought I'd have to drag you here by force."

Andrew was about to snort at the ridiculous idea of her forcing him to do anything when it occurred to him that although tiny, she might be stronger than him. He hadn't resisted when she'd pulled, but still, it had been one hell of a tug.

Did it make her any less appealing? Hell, no, quite the opposite. "You underestimate your charms, Dr. Bridget. There is nowhere I'd rather be than here, with you."

A lovely blush blossomed over her pale porcelain cheeks, and she glanced away. But that sly smile was still there when she returned her eyes to his face. "Quite the charmer, aren't you? I bet you make all the ladies swoon."

Andrew chuckled. "Hardly." He let her lead him to an examination table and sat down.

"Take off your jacket and your shirt," she said and reached for her stethoscope.

"What? Already? I was hoping for a nice dinner and a pleasant conversation before you got me to undress for you," he teased as he shrugged off his jacket, folded it, and put it beside him on the table, then tackled the buttons on his shirt.

Bridget smiled, the pink blush refusing to abandon her face. "I'll take you up on the offer of dinner and flirtatious chitchat, but first, I'm going to check you out." She winked, her blue eyes sparkling with mischief.

"I'm all yours, Doctor." Andrew shrugged his shirt off, making sure to suck in his gut and flex as he exposed his torso to her gaze. He was in good shape and carried no excess fat. Nevertheless, he didn't have the body of a twenty-year-old either. Not to mention the many scars—some small, some large—scattered over his chest and abdomen as well as his back. And the sparse hair on his chest wasn't enough to hide even the smaller ones.

Bridget let go of the stethoscope and let it hang around her neck. Getting closer, she reached with gentle fingers to touch an old bullet scar. "You lived dangerously, didn't you?" she whispered, trailing her fingers over some of the others.

Thank God, it hadn't been pity that he'd heard in her voice, more like admiration. Or at least he hoped it was the latter. "You could say so."

"You know, once you turn, your body would

probably heal these, even the older ones." She let her hand drop, but her eyes trailed over his front, making a tally, and she glanced behind him to look at the scars on his back.

"Would you like me better without them?" he teased, her scrutiny making him uncomfortable.

"I like you either way, with or without, how about that?" She plugged her ears and palmed the chest piece of the stethoscope. "Okay, breathe in... breathe out..."

He did as instructed, using the opportunity to sniff her hair as she leaned over him. Nice, some mild flowery scent, sweet and feminine, like Bridget herself. There was something very attractive about a soft, small woman that at the same time was a capable physician with a no-nonsense attitude and a strong personality.

"Perfect." She took the earpieces out and put the stethoscope away. "Okay, now shuck the pants."

"What? Why?" If Bridget was thinking about administering a prostate exam, she had another thing coming.

"Got you!" She giggled. "You should have seen your face... the sheer horror... Though come on, it's not like you have something I haven't seen before."

Devilish woman. "First of all, how do you know I don't?" He cocked a brow.

"Yeah, yeah, I'm sure you're hung like a horse..."

Bridget pushed at his chest to have him lie down. "And what's the second thing?"

"If I'm to let you poke me where the sun doesn't shine, it would only be after I've been naked in your bed first and have done some poking of my own."

Her cheeks pinked again. "My, oh my, what a naughty boy you are...," she murmured as she palpated his abdomen.

"You have no idea." He caught her hand and gave a tug, pulling her down on top of him. "Permission to kiss the doctor," he breathed a fraction of an inch away from her mouth.

"Permission granted," she said against his lips, then kissed him.

Tentative at first, it was no more than a brush of her lush lips against his, but as he closed his palm around her nape and drew her closer, she let out a moan and licked into his mouth.

His hands gentle as he caressed her back, Andrew wrestled with the urge to grab hold of Bridget and flip her under him. But she was so tiny compared to him, and he was afraid that letting out his hunger might overwhelm her.

Better let her set the pace.

Except, he wasn't sure how long his restraint would hold under Bridget's onslaught. She was kissing him and writhing on top of him with the abandon and urgency of a woman who knew exactly what she wanted and was starved of it. Her fingers seeking purchase on his short hair, she held him as she kissed him, her hips rocking over his hard shaft, setting him on fire.

"God, Bridget, I need you naked," he heard himself murmur against her lips as his arms tightened around her.

Fuck, he hadn't meant to say it out loud, and he hadn't meant to squash her to him either. But damn, it felt good— feeling her sweet little nipples getting so hard that they rubbed at his bare chest through her clothes. With a herculean effort, he eased his hold.

"Your wish is my command," she purred and reared up to her knees. Straddling his hips—her seductive smirk promised anything but demure obedience. She grabbed the hem of her red T-shirt and tugged it over her head, revealing creamy breasts covered by a sheer red bra that left nothing to the imagination. A moment later, it joined the shirt on the floor.

As if possessing a mind of their own, his hands reached and palmed the perky beauties.

"You're gorgeous."

She leaned into his touch, her eyes hooded. "Hold nothing back, Andrew, I'm a lot tougher than I look."

Okay...

She was under him in a flash.

"Better?" He smiled down at her before dipping his head to nuzzle her neck.

"Yes…" She arched into him, rubbing her breasts against his chest. "Oh, yes…just like that," she groaned as he slid down and licked around one nipple, then gasped as he sucked it in. "But it would be even better without the pants."

"Under one condition." He blew on her swollen, wet peak.

She arched a brow.

"The fuck-me red shoes stay on."

DARK ENEMY REDEEMED
Is available on Amazon
CLICK **HERE**

TRY THE SERIES ON

AUDIBLE

2 FREE audiobooks with your new Audible subscription!

FOR EXCLUSIVE PEEKS

Join The Children Of The Gods VIP Club
and gain access to the VIP portal at itlucas.com
click here to join

Included in your free membership:

- FREE narration of Goddess's Choice—Book 1 in The Children of the Gods Origins series.
- Preview chapters.
- And other exclusive content offered only to my VIPs.

Made in the USA
Lexington, KY
18 February 2019